Saint Cloud of Gaul:

The Prince Who Traded Kingdoms

Saint Cloud of Gaul:

The Prince Who Traded Kingdoms

A Novel

Susan Peek

Cover: Corinna Turner

Editor: Sandralena Hanley

ISBN-13: 978-0-9970005-9-7

Seven Swords Publications

www.SusanPeekAuthor.com

"In many chapels,

reddened by the setting sun,

the saints rest silently,

waiting for someone to love them."

These words, penned by an unknown priest, long dead,
were the inspiration for this series on the lives of saints
who have fallen deep into the shadows of obscurity.
My hope is that, in reading their heroic stories,
you will make the acquaintance of some of

God's Forgotten Friends

Susan Peek

To Sister Maria Philomena,

and all of her students, past, present, and to come.

And to Saint Cloud, of course,

with the prayer that he will find

"someone to love him."

6th Century France

Chapter One

Zephyr growled low, her black tail shooting between her legs as she stared out the open door. Danger lurked outside Cloud's hut. Or at least a stranger, which potentially meant the same thing. Cloud had no doubt, even after nearly a decade of hiding, that his uncles' assassins still hunted him. The two kings would never give up, not until they were certain Cloud's threat to their kingdoms was abolished forever.

In other words, until Cloud lay dead.

Trying to still the sudden slamming of his heart, Cloud closed his book of Gospels with a soft thump and snuffed out the flickering candle. The hut plunged into shadowy darkness, the only light a wedge of yellow moonbeam peeking through the open door. He eased from the rough-hewn table with the quiet stealth he'd perfected in the nine years since his childhood escape from being murdered, and tossed on the long black cloak, securing its hood over his head — always his first instinct to disguise his identity.

He slipped beside Zephyr at the door and kept his voice low. "What is it, Zeph? What's wrong?"

The puppy glanced up at him, then whimpered. She scooted backwards, away from the opening.

It took a moment for Cloud's eyes to adjust to the darkness.

When they did, he scanned the desolate marshland. The terrain sloped slightly downward at the edge of his soggy attempt at a vegetable patch, making it impossible to see beyond the row of trees. A warm wind swayed their branches. Apart from that, nothing unusual moved. No sound met Cloud's ears, except the continuous buzz of late summer mosquitoes and the garumph of a distant bullfrog.

"It's alright, Zeph. Nothing's out there." Cloud wasn't sure whom he was trying to convince, himself or the dog. He bent to ruffle Zephyr's black fur and was about to close the door when a slurping noise down the hill arrested his attention. Cloud froze. A boot stuck in mud? Cloud had experienced that himself many a time on his trek back to his hut after daily Mass at the chapel of Saint Clement. The slurping sounds were followed by snapping twigs, as if someone grappled with a bush to regain his balance in the squelchy mud.

More rustling noises. A splash, followed by a grunt. Muffled laughter, until someone hissed, "Shh!" so loudly it would have been humorous any other time.

But right now, Cloud could hardly breathe. It obviously wasn't Owun coming up, or Genofeva. Was it Tarquin, perhaps playing a joke on Cloud with a couple friends? Cloud still didn't know if he could trust him.

Or was this more than a joke? Had word of Cloud's whereabouts finally reached the castle?

Soft crunching indicated that the clumsy strangers, whomever they might be, had at last found the gravel path leading up the hill to his dwelling.

Zephyr bared her little teeth and growled again. A bead of sweat rolled between Cloud's shoulder blades, nothing to do this time with the sweltering hooded cloak he always wore. *Stay calm.* Zeph could be overreacting. She was young, hardly five months old, and not many people traveled this deep into the marshland. From a puppy's point of view, anything could be perceived as danger. The only humans Zephyr knew, after all, other than Cloud himself, were Tarquin, Genofeva, and Severin.

Severin! Cloud's thoughts raced to his mentor, and his heart stuttered in his chest. Severin was asleep and defenseless in the other hut, hardly more than a stone's throw behind Cloud's. If his uncles' henchmen were sneaking up in the dark — although with all their racket it hardly counted as sneaking — would they kill the holy hermit too? Surely even the most bloodthirsty warriors wouldn't hurt a frail and elderly priest!

Or . . . would they?

A faint glow rose from the slope and appeared between gnarled trees. Firelight danced. A torch.

A pair of lost travelers, possibly? But then why would one have warned the other with a shush?

If anything happened to Severin . . .

Two shadowy figures emerged. Firelight from the torch flickered around them and Cloud instantly spotted their loose flowing hair. Icy claws squeezed his chest. *Both men had long hair!*

Dear God, have mercy! This was worse than he thought. These were not merely his uncles' assassins. That would have been bad enough. But their cascading hair . . . it could only mean one thing.

Cloud's attention sped to their swords. The weapons were sheathed at the mens' sides, yes. But still! Fear curled Cloud's stomach. His dread was not so much for himself, but for the helpless priest asleep in the hut nearby.

His gaze lurched to his own weapon hanging on the wall across from the door. His father's sword. His grandfather's before that. The very sword Grandpere Clovis, the great King of the Franks, had wielded against the Alamanni in the Battle of Tolbiac, the miraculous victory which had led not only to

Grandpere's conversion, but had brought the whole nation of Gaul into the fold of Christ's true Church. The instinct to yank the giant sword down was nearly overpowering, and Cloud had to clench both fists around the material of his black cloak in order to quell the urge. The warrior blood coursing through his veins was not an easy thing to tame. Cloud had learned that only too well in his eighteen years of life.

But bloodshed was not the answer. It never had been. Not even in self-defense, if one were to live the Gospel message perfectly. What had Cloud been reading at the table a mere few minutes ago? Severin would be the first to insist that their safety rested solely in their Heavenly Father's loving care, not in the sharpness of a sword blade or the fighting skills — temporarily unused, but still there and oh so lethal — of a grandson of King Clovis. Cloud could picture the old hermit shaking his snowy-white head and telling Cloud, with his ever gentle smile, to put away the sword. The priest would have nothing to do with violence. Not even to save their lives.

Cloud forced himself to unclench his fists and release his breath. He lifted his right hand and desperately made the Sign of the Cross upon himself, pleading for the grace not to fight back, no matter what the next minutes would hold. Deep peace spread over him, as familiar to him as his penitential hooded cloak. He would not disappoint Severin, would not reach for Grandpere Clovis's sword. Its blade was already stained with far too much blood. The blood of his own brother Theodoald. The blood of Grandmere's cousin Sigismund, revered as a saint, yet brutally slain by Cloud's own father. No, Cloud would not allow himself to turn into the heartless and bloodthirsty monster that his father had been . . . and his approaching uncles still were.

After whispering a *Pater Noster* for courage to die bravely, should death tonight be God's will, Cloud did something he had not done since that fateful afternoon nine years ago. He reached up and pulled off the hood of his black cloak, finally allowing his long blond hair to tumble loose.

Shaking it out, he let it fall in kingly splendor over his shoulders, matching that of the royal pair closing in. He would meet the killers on the killers' terms. The two kings sought a prince. A prince they would find.

Dragging a breath, Cloud gathered his courage and stepped out the door, unarmed, to face his doom.

Nine Years Earlier

Chapter Two

If Cloud had realized the soldiers would lock them in the empty room, he would not have followed his brothers inside. He would have fled. Shouted for help. Anything but go in. But how was he to know?

Hardly had he stepped inside behind Theodoald and Gunther when the massive oak door thudded shut behind them. With an ominous clunk, the steel bolt on the outside slammed into place. Cloud spun in alarm.

"Why did Uncle Childebert's men just lock us in?"

Gunther was ten, a whole year older than Cloud, and usually knew everything. Not this time. His attention flicked to the towering door, and he frowned. "I don't know," he said, for the first time in his life.

In unison, they looked at Theodoald. Their older brother must not have heard the lock bang into place. He'd made his way to the room's one window, his royal purple cloak already dumped unceremoniously on the floor next to him as he gazed outside. A strong breeze whipped his long red-blond hair. Cloud couldn't see his expression, but by the way Theodoald bounced on his toes, Cloud could imagine him bubbling with excitement.

"Would you look at that. I've never seen such a wild forest in my life." Theodoald let out an impressed whistle and swiveled around. "This is so much better than Grandmere's land." A grin split his face. "Do you think there could be bears around here? How much you wanna bet I can shoot one?"

Cloud suppressed a sigh. All Theodoald talked about since he'd turned twelve was hunting with the bow and arrow Grandmere Clothilde had given him for his birthday.

Gunther said, "They locked us in."

Theodoald didn't seem to register the words. "Imagine bringing down a bear! And we don't even have to ask permission to go hunting anymore!" His eyes glowed. "We can do whatever we want from now on. By this afternoon, we'll be kings. Actual *kings*!"

Cloud flicked his own blond strands out of his eyes with annoyance. Grandmere had insisted they wear their hair down today, flowing loose and long in all its royal glory, as befit their princely rank. As far as Cloud was concerned, it just got in the way. "Didn't you hear what Gunther said? Uncle Childebert's soldiers locked us in."

"Huh?" Theodoald's grin faded slightly. "Locked us in?" He looked at the door. "Are you sure?"

"We heard the bolt." As if to prove it, Gunther strode back and yanked on the iron handle with both hands. It didn't budge.

The remainder of Theodoald's grin fled, a puzzled frown taking its place. He leaned back against the ledge of the open window and crossed his arms. "That makes no sense. Why would they lock us in?"

"You tell us." The first trace of fear edged Gunther's voice. He pulled again at the handle.

Cloud said, "I thought we're supposed to be at a ceremony, making us kings."

Gunther gave up and turned away from the door, his face paling. "That's what Senator Arcadius told us in the carriage."

For a moment Theodoald stared warily at the door. Then he

blinked and shook his head. "Calm down, you two. I'm sure nothing's wrong. Maybe the ceremony's running late or something." He bit his lip. "Uncle Clothaire's here too, right? Grandmere never would have sent us to Uncle Childebert's castle if she didn't trust them." But his voice shook slightly when he said it.

For some reason, goosebumps marched up Cloud's arms. An alarm started to clang in his head. He scanned the room, searching for an escape route, should one be needed. The open window was the only possibility, but it looked awfully small.

He'd thought it strange all along that the three of them had been separated so quickly from the retinue that accompanied them to Uncle Childebert's castle. Grandmere Clothilde had insisted on an escort, personally picking a handful of soldiers, a tutor, and a couple of monks to travel with them. But they'd ridden in separate carriages and Cloud hadn't seen any of them since arriving. He swallowed, trying to replay in his head the conversation he'd overheard between Grandmere and Senator Arcadius, who'd arrived unannounced at her palace in Lutece this morning.

"My lady, I bring an urgent message from your most noble sons, King Clothaire and King Childebert," Arcadius had said when a servant ushered him into the courtyard. Grandmere was picking autumn blooms, as she often did for the church altar. As usual, Cloud and Gunther were tagging along, carrying her basket and clippers. Any excuse to get out of their lessons.

Grandmere Clothilde had looked up from the bush bursting with orange flowers, the one beside the stone fountain, her brows lifted in surprise. Cloud got the impression she hadn't been expecting any message from his uncles. They rarely spoke to her, after all. Except when they wanted something. Everyone knew that.

"They bid thee send them the three boys immediately, that

they may be made kings."

Grandmere flinched. The color drained from her cheeks.

"I realize it's very sudden, my lady. Forgive the haste, but your sons wish to honor their nephews by giving them their late father's throne. A carriage is waiting."

Cloud looked at Gunther and wondered if his own eyes had grown as wide as his brother's. They'd always known that someday they would inherit Father's kingdom of Orleans. But . . . today? Right now? With no warning?

Grandmere groped for a second before sinking onto the edge of the stone fountain. The freshly picked bouquet dropped from her hand. That's when the servant who'd brought Arcadius into the garden shooed Cloud and Gunther away. Neither of them heard the rest of the conversation.

After that, the morning passed in a blur. Servants scrambled. Clothes were whipped out of trunks. Everyone darted about in a frenzy. And all along, Cloud could tell that Grandmere Clothilde was fighting panic. He felt it in the tremble of her hands when she'd brushed his long hair and fiddled to fasten the fancy brooch on his gold-spun tunic. She couldn't even remember where the servants had placed the boys' purple cloaks, when all along they lay draped on a chair right behind her. Grandmere never acted like that. To make things worse, she kept glancing at the crucifix on the wall, her lips quivering, as if in silent prayer. Cloud had never seen her so agitated. More than once it seemed she'd changed her mind and would refuse to let the three of them out of her care.

But the senator was so insistent. Besides, what could Grandmere do against the power of the two kings? So before Cloud knew it, he and his brothers were piled into one carriage with Arcadius, while their retine was herded into others. Wringing her hands, Grandmere had tried to be brave. Her last words were, "My children, I shall not think that I have lost my son, your father, if I live to see you reign from his throne." She reached up to give them each a hug — so tight that Cloud could hardly breathe — then they were rumbling away to Paris to be made kings.

So why were they imprisoned in this stone room instead of sitting in the Great Hall, feasting on venison and sweetmeats, jeweled crowns balanced atop their heads?

Theodoald cleared his throat, the way he did when he was nervous. "Did anyone see either of our uncles when we entered the castle?"

"No," Gunther said. "Not me." He turned to Cloud. "Did you?"

Cloud shook his head, dread clawing up his spine.

"You don't think it's a trap, do you, Theodoald?" Gunther kept his voice a whisper, as if speaking loudly might give truth to his words.

Fear tightened Cloud's chest. He didn't want to admit it, but both uncles frightened him. They were big and fierce and scowled all the time. Their sword blades were always stained with flecks of dried blood, as if they had killed so many people it would never completely wash off. Even Grandmere Clothilde was scared of them, and they were her own sons.

Theodoald sucked in a breath. "Grandmere would've known if it was a trap." His Adam's apple bobbed. "I . . . I think we're worrying over nothing."

Cloud didn't think so. He'd lived barely a decade, yet every year had been drenched in blood. First Cousin Sigismund's grisly murder. Then Father's death in battle a year later. Horrible memories chased each other across Cloud's mind. Cousin Godomar parading Father's head around the countryside on a pike. Aunt Clotilda's mangled, lifeless body in Grandmere Clothilde's arms, unrecognizable after what that Visigoth brute, her husband down south, had done to her. Mother being dragged away, sobbing and begging, by Uncle Clothaire — never to be seen by Cloud or his brothers again. Battles and bloodshed and treachery and terror . . . that's all Cloud had ever known. Apart from the hours he spent with Grandmere, strolling in her peaceful gardens, accompanying her to Mass and her visits to the poor, and his tutoring sessions with the kind priests, Cloud's existence was marked by violence. So were his brothers'. They had every reason to be worried, locked in a room of stone by men whose hands and hearts were soaked with blood.

"Someone's coming!" Gunther leaped away from the door so suddenly it made Cloud jump.

Footfalls clomped in the corridor, then halted ominously outside the door. All three boys froze. Iron scraped against iron as the bolt was wrenched from its socket. Cloud tried to slow the galloping of his heart as the heavy door groaned open.

Uncle Childebert strode into the room, Uncle Clothaire a pace behind. They definitely weren't dressed for a banquet. The long hallway behind them stretched empty, not another soul in sight.

Theodoald jerked up straight from his leaning position against the window ledge.

Uncle Clothaire's blubbery lips twisted into a sickening smile. "Do you miss your dead father? Do you ever wish you could see him again?"

Cloud frowned. So did Gunther. They glanced uncertainly at their older brother.

Theodoald hesitated, obviously unsure how to answer the strange question. "Uh . . ." His eyes met Cloud's for a moment, then he looked back at their uncle. "I . . . I guess so."

"Well, isn't that fortunate?" Uncle Clothaire laughed and whipped out his sword. "Because you're all about to join him."

Chapter Three

Cloud froze. Gunther gasped. Theodoald lunged across the room to protect them.

He didn't make it. Uncle Clothaire sprang forward and with one swift thrust impaled him. The sword plunged so hard the blade came out Theodoald's back.

His eyes popped wide with soundless agony as a rush of bright blood flooded down his gold-spun tunic and sprayed the walls. He staggered a few steps, his movements slow and grotesque, before hitting the stone floor with a thud. Cloud watched in stunned horror. For a fraction of a second, their eyes locked, Theodoald's imploring. Blood pumped over his hands as he groped blindly at the hilt, as if trying to pull the sword out. Then, with a shuddering thrash, he stilled.

No! A sob of anguish tore from Cloud's throat. *No, no! This couldn't be happening!* He dived to his knees beside Theodoald, his heart exploding with shock. Somewhere in the back of his mind, he was aware of screaming. It must be Gunther. The high-pitched guttural sound split his ears.

Uncle Clothaire sidestepped Cloud and Theodoald on the floor, as if they were annoying pieces of furniture around which to navigate. Somehow a long dagger had appeared in his hand. He headed towards Gunther. "Age order. You're next, brat."

Gunther's screams shattered the air. He scrambled behind their other uncle, as if for protection.

Uncle Clothaire kept coming. He was going to kill Gunther! Cloud had to stop him! *The sword. Grab the sword!*

Cloud didn't want to look at Theodoald's contorted face, didn't want to see his open, sightless eyes. And more than anything, he didn't want to touch that awful sword sticking out of his brother's body. But Gunther was about to be murdered! With no idea how he would fight off two strong men, Cloud forced himself to close his hands around the hilt. He nearly gagged.

A few feet away, Gunther was on his knees now, clasping Uncle Childebert's legs for dear life. "Don't kill us!" he sobbed. Raw terror laced his voice. "Uncle Childebert, save me! Please! Don't let him kill me!"

Uncle Clothaire towered above Gunther, the dagger raised in his huge hairy hand.

Fighting down the bile in his throat, Cloud clenched both hands around the sword's hilt. He yanked with all his might.

It didn't budge.

"Clothaire, maybe this isn't right after all. They're only children. They're —"

"This was your idea. You're the one who planned this." Anger flared in Uncle Clothaire's voice. He turned from Gunther and seared Uncle Childebert with a glare. "It was you who lured them here to your castle. Are you turning coward on me?"

His uncles were arguing. Gunther was whimpering. For the moment, no one paid attention to Cloud. He scrambled to his feet and tossed his blood-streaked royal cloak over one shoulder, out of the way. Hating himself for the heartless motion, Cloud planted a boot against Theodoald's chest. He heaved the sword with all his strength. It moved slightly. He grit his teeth and pulled harder. With a sickening sound — half squelching, half grating — the sword dislodged. Cloud stumbled back as his weight shifted and the crimson blade lurched free.

"There are other ways to secure the kingdom of Orleans. We don't have to kill them."

"A little late for that, brother."

"We can lock these two in the dungeon. They'll never be found. If we hide Theodoald's body and pretend there was an accident, we might be able to — "

"They're Clodomir's heirs, you fool! The only way to get his throne is to eliminate them!"

Still unnoticed, Cloud hefted the massive sword. It weighed more than he expected. Trembling, he re-positioned his hands around the bloodied hilt, his legs all but crumpling beneath him from fear. What was he going to do with the sword now that he had it? He could never fight them off. They were men. He was nine years old. How could he ever —

Suddenly he spotted the engravings on the blade beneath the blood. His lungs froze.

"The nobles will never suspect we killed him . . ."

The crest of Grandpere Clovis was engraved on the metal! Nausea lurched Cloud's stomach. He was going to throw up. Uncle Clothaire had murdered Theodoald with their father's own sword, the one he'd inherited from Grandpere!

"No one will know. No one will —" A sharp *whap* cut off Uncle Childebert's words.

Cloud's gaze jerked to his uncles. A red splotch appeared on Uncle Childebert's cheek, where Uncle Clothaire must have whacked him with the hilt of the dagger. Uncle Childebert nearly lost his balance, stumbling a few steps from the impact. Uncle Clothaire swiftly moved in front of him, face to face, and grabbed him by the collar. His neck veins bulged in rage. "Kill the brats. I did the first. The other two are yours. That was the deal."

Uncle Childebert turned away in disgust. Uncle Clothaire kept step with him, getting in his face again. Gunther still clung to Uncle Childebert's legs, being dragged around the floor as their two uncles moved. A strangled sob escaped from his throat and Cloud caught his terrified expression. He had to save Gunther, *now,* while their uncles were distracted with their argument. Did they even realize he was standing behind them holding Father's sword? He inched closer, his pulse thundering in his ears.

"No." Uncle Childebert's voice wavered. "I won't do it. They're innocent."

Rage flamed through Uncle Clothaire and he screamed, "This whole thing was your plan! You're the one who thought of it! Kill them or I'll kill *you*!"

"You're a monster." Uncle Childebert shook Gunther off his legs and stepped out of the way. "Kill them yourself."

Adrenaline surged through Cloud and he flung himself towards Uncle Clothaire with the sword.

Too late. Steel flashed, swift as lightning, and Uncle Clothaire slammed the dagger into Gunther's neck, then swung towards Cloud. He eyed the sword. "Oh, I see. You want to fight me, do you?" He laughed.

Terror rushed through Cloud. He backed away. Panic clamped his lungs. There was no escape! There was nowhere that he could —

His gaze snagged the window. He bolted.

"Grab him!"

Gripping the sword for dear life, Cloud leaped over Theodoald's body and dived for the window.

"Don't let him escape!"

Footsteps skidded behind him on the stones. It sounded like someone slipped in the pooling blood. Cloud didn't dare look behind. He was nearly at the window…

A hand grabbed him. Cloud swerved. The grip slid away.

He reached the open window. Hoisting the heavy sword, he threw it outside. The weapon disappeared, clattering against the wall, landing in the grass a few feet below. Breath coming in panicked gasps, Cloud scrambled onto the ledge and jammed himself into the hole. His royal purple cloak snagged on a jagged stone and he twisted his head to free it. His forehead banged against the frame and red points of light flashed behind his eyelids. Pain exploded in his skull. A hand snapped around one ankle and yanked his foot so hard it felt like his leg would be ripped off.

Blood pounded in his temples but his vision cleared. He kicked backwards with both legs as hard as he could. His foot smashed into something. There was a crack — someone's nose maybe? — followed by a yelp of pain. His foot was released. Cursing filled the air.

Wrenching his cloak free, so hard that it tore, Cloud wriggled through the opening, begging God that he wouldn't get stuck. God heard his prayers. With a final squirm, he cleared the window and plunged to the ground, a purple balloon billowing behind him. With a clunk, he landed on his shoulder, his face smothered by the purple material of his cloak. Pain ricocheted through his arm. He bit back a cry. For a moment he lay there in agony, tears stinging his eyes.

A torrent of curses poured from the window a few feet above.

He had to get away! Forcing himself to ignore the fire in his shoulder, he untangled himself from the folds of his cloak and rolled to his knees. He searched the ground frantically. Father's sword. Where was it? *Hurry!*

Over there, a few feet to his left. Cloud scrabbled across the grass on all fours and lunged for it, still hearing curses of rage above him. His trembling fingers closed around the hilt. Using both hands, he pulled it towards him and staggered clumsily to his feet.

There was only one place to go. The woods.

He threw a glance upward at the window. Uncle Clothaire's face poked through, one hand clasped over his nose, blood pouring down his face. He was so angry he shook with fury. For a moment Cloud could only stare in fear. Then he spun around to run.

And slammed straight into a body.

Chapter Four

The force of the collision propelled Cloud backwards. His legs shot out from under him and he tumbled back to the ground. The person he'd crashed into equally lost his balance and ended up sprawled on top of Cloud. There was an awkward tangle of limbs and long hair and hunting gear. Something that looked suspiciously like a dead badger went sailing from the other's grip and flew through the air.

"Grab him!" a voice shouted above their heads.

Cloud blinked, scooting backwards in the grass, trying to free himself and regain his feet.

"Cloud? What on earth —"

Oh no! It was Charibert, Uncle Clothaire's son! He must have been out hunting. Thus the flying badger. His eyes were popped wide, confusion stamped on his face. He shoved his long straggly curls from his eyes. "Cloud? Are you alright? Why did you jump out the window?"

"Don't let him escape!" Uncle Clothaire screamed.

Charibert was slightly older than Theodoald and the two were best friends. Or rather, had been best friends until a few minutes ago, because now Theodoald was dead. Charibert was big for his age, and strong, which usually made people think he was older than he was. For a fleeting second Cloud wondered if his cousin would protect him. But even if Charibert wanted to, what could he do? Nothing. Absolutely nothing. Cloud's only chance was to run.

Clambering to his feet, he risked a glance upward. Both kings stood framed together in the window, Uncle Clothaire's face contorted in fury as blood streamed from his nose. Next to him, Uncle Childebert's face was sickly gray and his forehead glistened with sweat.

Cloud stumbled a pace, lugging the crimson sword, then bolted towards the woods as best as he could with the heavy weapon.

"Chase him, you fool! *Chase him!*"

"Wha—? Why?"

Not waiting to see if Charibert would obey his father, Cloud sprinted. Tears blinded him. He swerved this way and that through the trees, trying to lose anyone who might give chase. Fear gave wings to his feet.

Dodging overhanging branches, skittering around bushes, and sloshing at breakneck speed through the stagnant puddles from last week's rain, he had no idea how far he ran. Grief and panic made it hard to breathe, but terror and adrenaline spurred him on.

Finally, after what seemed forever, exhaustion won out and Cloud collapsed, breathless and trembling, to his knees. He dropped Father's sword on the carpet of crinkly dead leaves and gasped for air. He couldn't pull enough into his lungs. Hot tears burned his eyes; it felt like his heart — and his life — had exploded into a thousand pieces. Theodoald was dead. Gunther was dead. *How could this be happening?*

And what about Charibert? Was he following? If he overtook Cloud, he might drag him back to the castle, having no idea about the murders.

Cloud forced himself to grow still, listening. It wasn't easy to be quiet with his breath heaving. The caw of a crow shattered the silence, startling him. Unseen creatures twittered and scurried in the undergrowth. A chilly breeze rustled the trees above him, sending a fresh flurry of orange and red leaves to the ground. But he detected no sounds of human pursuit.

Yet.

Cloud knew his uncles would hunt him down. They had no choice now but to kill him; he was witness to their terrible crime. And just because Charibert hadn't chased him immediately didn't mean the older boy wouldn't soon set out. Cloud realized with sudden horror that he'd blazed a trail through the woods that anyone with half a brain could follow. Broken branches, footprints in the dirt, smushed leaves on the ground with bloody drippings from the sword blade.

He sank down in exhaustion and hugged his arms around himself, shuddering. Fear churned his stomach. Did Grandmere's retinue, who'd ridden in the other carriages, know what happened? Was word of the murders flying even now through the castle? Surely *someone* had heard Gunther's desperate screams. He'd shrieked loud enough to wake the dead. Maybe soldiers — *good ones!* — were already scouring the woods, searching for Cloud to rescue him. Dare he stay still and wait for them to find him?

He bit his lip, trying to decide. Staying here seemed risky. Nothing guaranteed Grandmere's men would find him before his uncles did. The only place he'd be truly safe was back at Grandmere's castle. But how could he get there? Lutece was miles away. Cloud had no idea how long it would take him to walk. Days? Longer if he got lost, which was a real possibility since he didn't know the way. He was lost *already*! And what would he eat? Where would he sleep? The nights were cold. And to top off everything, Theodoald said these woods could be teaming with bears.

Panic mounting, he looked around him. Dense, shadowy woods closed in on all sides. Afternoon had already given way to early evening. Giant trees towered towards the sky, shrouding the forest in gloom, leaving only mottled patches of sunlight on the mossy, leaf-strewn ground. There were no paths to follow, no landmarks to guide his steps.

Cloud swallowed. Well, he'd better keep moving before darkness fell. Shakily, he stood up and hoisted the sword.

Jesus, please let me find somewhere safe to stay the night.

He began walking. Deeper and deeper into the sinister woods.

He had no idea how long he trudged. An hour? Two? Finally, right when he felt he would collapse from tiredness, he sighted a rundown hut.

Hope rose and he started running towards the building. Maybe it was abandoned and he could spend the night there!

His hopes were dashed when he spotted the faint glow of a lantern in a window. Someone was home.

Now what? He wanted to cry.

Blessed Mother, please help me! I'm so tired and scared. I need to hide somewhere!

God's Mother had a way of listening, just like Grandmere Clothilde always said she would. A mere second later, Cloud saw the woodshed.

Chapter Five

Cloud groggily stirred. The sensation of warm, moist breath tickled his ear. He ignored it, bone tired, and instantly drifted off to sleep again.

The panting continued. Then a soft growly noise. Right next to his head.

A bear!

Eyes shooting open in the dark, Cloud frantically fumbled for Father's sword, as memories rushed over him. His panicked trek through the woods last night, stumbling upon this tiny shed, curling up in fear and exhaustion against the cold stack of rough logs. He must have dozed off. And now — a bear was breathing in his face!

The sword — it was missing! The hilt must have slipped from his grip when he'd fallen asleep! Before his eyes could adjust to the dim light, something wet and slobbery slid across his cheek. He sat upright in terror.

A soft ball bounded into his lap. The thing squirmed up his chest, a smudge of white in the darkness.

Relief surged as Cloud realized it wasn't a bear after all. It was only a little dog with a fiercely wagging tail, trying to lick his face. Its warm fur brought unexpected consolation and Cloud nearly laughed.

"Well, hello there. How did you get inside?" Cloud pulled the dog into his lap for a cuddle. But his relief lasted all of three seconds. A gasp near the shed door made Cloud jump out of his skin.

He swiveled towards the sound. A girl with messy blonde braids stood frozen at the entrance, silhouetted against the first peeking rays of morning sunlight. She was small; perhaps his own age. Her feet were bare and her dress ragged and unshapely. But beneath the layers of dirt smudged on her face, Cloud couldn't help notice she was pretty.

Recovering from her obvious surprise, she turned her head and yelled into the yard, "Owun! Come quick!"

"I'm busy," a voice called back. "What do you want?"

"Bree found a girl sleeping in the shed!"

A girl? There was a girl sleeping in here too? Confused, Cloud looked around. The shed was too tiny. No one else could fit. He was the only one inside. Just him and this little white dog, whom he guessed must be Bree.

Then it hit him. Girls had long hair, boys had short.

With one exception only. Royalty.

Oh no! They would figure out who he was! Shoving the dog off his lap, Cloud grappled for the sword, ungracefully heaved it up with both hands, and jumped to his feet. Not that the little girl was a threat. But maybe unseen Owun was.

Cloud's sudden action must have startled the girl, for she gasped again and leaped away from the door. "Bree! Come here, girl! Get away from her!" she begged. But the dog didn't obey. It let out a playful bark and nipped at Cloud's leg.

A boy, several years older, came into view. He was holding a bucket. "What's going on, Genofeva?"

"Careful, Owun! She has a sword!"

"What on earth?" Sounding amused, the boy stepped next to her and thrust his head into the shed. Cloud cringed. It seemed to him as if the purple of his cloak filled the whole space. Everything about him — his flowing hair, his royal cloak and fancy clothes, his massive weapon — screamed one word: *Prince.*

The amusement hovered on the boy's features for a second, then dissolved into shock, which quickly morphed into disbelief. He nearly dropped the bucket, causing water to slosh everywhere, and thudded to the ground on one knee.

"Forgive us," he blundered, bowing his head. "We . . . we didn't realize . . ." His sentence helplessly faded. He reached behind him and yanked the hem of the girl's dress, whispering way too loudly, "Genofeva, curtsy!"

"Huh? Why?"

Owun jerked her down and she crashed to her knees next to him. Irritation flashed across her features and she instantly popped up again. Flinging one braid out of her face, she slapped the dirt and dead leaves off her dress and looked from Cloud to Owun with obvious defiance. "It's just a girl. She has no right to be in our shed. Who does she think she is? Besides, I only kneel for God!"

Despite himself, a smile leaked through Cloud's lips at her last sentence. He lowered the sword and said to Owun, "It's alright. You can stand up too."

Owun raised his head. Hesitation swept his face. Surely he wondered what a prince was doing in his family's woodshed.

"You can get up," Cloud repeated. "Really."

Owun obeyed, but his eyes seemed to be calculating, trying to figure the situation out. Was he a threat? He looked at least fifteen. He could easily overpower Cloud, even with the sword, if for any reason he chose to. And what about their parents? Would they turn Cloud over to his uncles if they found him lurking in their yard? Judging from the spilled bucket, Owun had been fetching water while Genofeva came for firewood.

Hopefully their parents had remained inside.

A sudden frown furrowed Genofeva's brow. "Wait." She glanced at Owun, then back at Cloud. "It's a boy." Her eyes bugged. "It's a boy! *No way!*"

"Genofeva, would you just —"

"What is he doing sneaking around our place, frightening people with that horrible sword?"

"Genofeva, shush." Red snuck up Owun's neck in obvious embarrassment. "Forgive my sister, my lord. Unfortunately, her tongue is swifter than her brain."

"It is not!" She shoved her brother, then skewered Cloud with a glare.

But the glare faded, then vanished altogether. "Wait. Did you just call him — "

"He's a prince. How dense are you? Now shut your mouth."

Genofeva did more than that. She clamped both hands over it with a startled squeal. Then she curtsied so quickly she almost lost her balance. Color shot to her cheeks. "I'm so sorry, I'm so sorry, my lord prince." She threw a pleading look at her brother, eyes wide. "Is that what we call him? *My lord prince*?" Before Owun could answer, she blurted to Cloud, "Why did you spend the night in our shed when you've got a whole fancy castle to sleep in? I'd kill to sleep in a castle!"

Her innocence disarmed him. Everything inside Cloud longed to spill the whole story, to trust someone. Maybe they would even help him. "I'm . . ." Cloud hesitated, but the words escaped before he had a chance to weigh them. "I'm . . . um, hiding."

Owun's eyebrows lifted. "Hiding?"

"Please don't tell anyone I'm here." Cloud swallowed. "Or, more importantly, who I am."

Genofeva squished up her face. "How can we tell anyone who you are when we don't know ourselves?"

"My name's Cloud. I'm the son of King Clodomir of Orleans."

As soon as he identified his father, he regretted it. Father had been known as a monster, just like Uncle Clothaire and Uncle Childebert. Surely Owun and Genofeva knew the shocking story of King Sigismund the Saint, who'd been brutally tortured and beheaded by Father's sword — the very same sword Cloud held in his hands right now. For a terrible moment he held his breath, realizing he'd gone too far. They'd be scared of him now. They'd judge him and hate him for his dead father's crimes. He cringed, waiting for their reaction.

But their expressions remained blank. Neither of them so much as blinked, as if the name King Clodomir meant nothing to them. Huh. Maybe news of kings and torture and sickening royal crimes didn't reach the peasants. Or maybe they were both too young to remember. In any case, *thank You, God.*

Cloud took a relieved breath and continued. "Yesterday my two brothers, Theodoald and Gunther . . ." He had to pause, hot tears suddenly stinging his eyes. "They . . . were murdered. At the castle. I saw it happen."

Owun recoiled. Genofeva's mouth dropped.

"My uncles tried to kill me next, but I got away. If they find me . . ." — involuntary shaking took hold of him — "they're going to murder me too."

A sudden noise beyond the shed made Owun spin around in alarm. Bree barked and Genofeva swiveled her head so quickly that her braids swung in a wide arc. Leaves crinkled and twigs cracked wildly as someone approached.

"Hey, you two. Who's in that shed?"

Owun's color drained.

"No one," Genofeva blurted, but her body went stiff, as with fear.

"Don't lie. Anyone can see you're talking to someone in

there."

Cloud stumbled backwards, pulse racing, and flattened himself so quickly against the woodpile that several logs tumbled down. He winced at the racket.

Genofeva turned back to him with unmistakable panic and their eyes locked. "Do all kings have long hair, like you?" she asked in a tiny whisper.

The blood chilled in Cloud's veins.

He swallowed and nodded.

"I'm so sorry, my lord prince." Ghostly white, she bit her lip. "He's going to kill you. He has a sword."

Chapter Six

Cloud pressed himself as tightly as he could against the stack of logs, begging the shadows to swallow him. He willed himself to disappear, to turn invisible. He knew it wouldn't happen.

Was it Uncle Clothaire out there, or Uncle Childebert? Given a choice, he'd prefer Uncle Childebert. Not that it mattered. He was already good as dead. The sword in his hand was useless. He could never fight either uncle off. But Uncle Childebert might kill him quicker, and therefore be more merciful. If it was Uncle Clothaire, he'd probably find it amusing to torture Cloud first, as punishment for his escape, and then kill him using Father's sword, just as he'd done to Theodoald.

Sweat slicked Cloud's palms. What would it feel like to be tortured, then skewered with a sword? Would it take a long time? Would it hurt? Theodoald died quickly but in agony. Cloud hadn't stayed around long enough to witness Gunther's last breath; for all he knew, his brother had writhed in pain on the floor for ages. Fear cramped his stomach. *Please God, let it be Uncle Childebert.*

Unexpectedly, an image of Grandmere Clothilde flashed through his mind. Sadness would all but kill her too when she learned of his death, and the deaths of his brothers. The thought of her crying was awful, but her faith was stronger than anyone's

Cloud knew, so she would somehow be alright in the end. Cloud tried to picture what she would say to him, if she was miraculously in this shed and watching her bloodthirsty son approach outside.

Don't be scared, Cloud. God is with you.

Or maybe, *Heaven will be worth it.*

And definitely, *Make a sincere act of contrition. Tell Jesus you love Him, and ask Him not to go to Purgatory.*

She'd say stuff like that. Consoling and calm, despite her sorrow.

So that's what Cloud must do. He squeezed his eyes closed and tried to pray, to say the things Grandmere would have him say. He was too frightened to move his hand to make the Sign of the Cross, but he was sure she'd say that God would understand.

Footfalls stopped right at the spot where Cloud knew Genofeva was standing. Or rather *had* been standing, because she wouldn't be standing there anymore. She'd be replaced by one of his evil uncles. He imagined her and Owun, their expressions horrified and helpless, obediently stepping out of the way of the king with the massive sword. Unable to watch his doom unfold, Cloud kept his eyes tightly shut and struggled to breathe. Forget the prayers. His mind went numb with fear.

He heard Genofeva whisper, "Please don't kill him. Please don't." Her tone was pleading.

"Geesh, Cloud. I've been looking for you all night."

Cloud's eyes shot open.

No bloodthirsty uncle stood at the door. It was Charibert. His long hair was windblown, his eyes red and puffy, as if he'd been crying. Charibert never cried. But Theodoald had been his best friend. Maybe he'd seen the bodies.

"I was so afraid my father would find you first. Thank God I did." Charibert wasn't very religious, but the way he said it, it sure sounded like a genuine prayer of gratitude. Dizzy with relief, Cloud sagged against the wood pile. It felt like the weight of a thousand pounds dropped off his shoulders.

"Soldiers are hunting for you everywhere." His cousin's voice broke. "It's terrible at the castle. I . . . I can't even describe it. My father and Uncle Childebert murdered so many people."

Genofeva clapped a hand over her mouth in horror. Cloud jerked up straight, feeling like he'd been punched in the gut. "*What?*"

"They killed all the men Grandmere sent with you, so that they couldn't come and rescue you. It . . . it was a bloodbath."

Cloud stared at his cousin, horror-struck. His head felt light. He had to steady himself against the woodpile.

"My father thinks I'm looking for you to turn you in." Charibert indicated the sword in his hand. "Or more precisely, to kill you."

Beyond the door, Owun visibly tensed, as if ready for a fight should Charibert make an unexpected move. But Charibert said, "I could never kill you, Cloud." He threw an anxious glance into the surrounding woods. "I need to get you to safety."

Genofeva asked in a tiny voice, "What are we going to do?"

Somehow, in the last few minutes, it had become *we*. Not just Cloud. Not just Cloud and Charibert. But all four of them.

Charibert must have sensed it too. He didn't even seem to care who Genofeva and Owun were or how they had become involved. He simply took charge. He turned to Owun and asked, "Can you use a sword?"

Owun hesitated, then shook his head. "I don't think so, my lord."

Charibert sighed. "Then at least carry it." He reached out and took the heavy weapon from Cloud, then held it towards Owun. "We can move faster without Cloud having to lug it around." Owun accepted the weapon and wonder filled his eyes as he spotted its intricate engraving.

In any other circumstance, Cloud would have burned with the stinging insult of a peasant having to carry his sword. But right now, he was only too grateful for the protection of the two older boys. His cousin was only a few years older than Theodoald had been, but tall and strong for his age. He was certainly trained to use a sword. And Owun looked like he could hold his own in a hand-to-hand fight, if weapons weren't involved.

Charibert studied him for a moment. "What's your name?"

Owun was staring at the sword in his hands with awe, obviously fascinated by the crest engraved on the blade. He'd probably never seen a weapon crafted so finely. Anyone could tell it was the sword of a king.

"Hey, I asked you a question. What's your name?"

Owun's head jerked up. "Owun, my lord. Forgive me, this sword is just so —"

He didn't get to finish his sentence because Genofeva piped in. "I'm Genofeva. Can I hold it, Owun?"

Both boys ignored her.

"Where are your parents?"

Owun said, "Inside, my lord."

"Do they know Cloud's here?'

Owun and Genofeva both shook their heads.

Charibert said, "Don't breathe a word to them. They're safer knowing nothing. My father would behead them in a heartbeat." Leaving them to absorb that grisly tidbit, he turned to Cloud. "A woodshed? Seriously? What a pathetic place to hide."

Cloud couldn't help but think Theodoald would say the same thing.

"No one found me here."

Charibert snorted. "I did."

"Wait!" Genofeva blurted, practically leaping in the air. Everyone looked at her. "I know the perfect place he can hide! Somewhere that nobody will *ever* think of. It's a secret room in a field."

Owun gave her a doubtful look. "A secret room? In a *field*?" He rolled his eyes. "Don't play games, Genofeva. This is serious."

She glared at him. "I *am* being serious. Bree and I found it a couple years ago." She gave a little shudder, then reached down to scoop up the dog. She held Bree tightly against her chest. "It was really spooky. But I think I might be able to find it again."

Charibert shot a worried look at the nearby hut and ran his fingers through his hair. "We need to hurry."

Genofeva hesitated. She looked at Cloud with something like apology. "I . . . um, I don't know if it's safe though. I have no idea what's down there."

Down there? For some reason, goosebumps prickled Cloud's spine. This *definitely* did not sound consoling.

Chapter Seven

"I think it's somewhere around here." Genofeva balled the hem of her ragged dress in one hand and climbed ungracefully over a boulder. Bree bounded ahead of her, dipping from view in the tall brown grass, then reappearing, every few seconds. "I think it was near those bushes over there."

Cloud followed, Charibert beside him. They swerved clumsily around the giant strewn rocks littering the secluded field. The waist-deep weeds and uneven footing made the trek surprisingly treacherous. More than once, all three stumbled. Cloud understood now why Genofeva claimed no one would find him out here. He couldn't imagine anyone being stupid enough to risk breaking a leg. He felt sorry for Genofeva in her bare feet. Should he offer her his boots? She didn't even have a cloak to protect her from the chilly air. More than once, he almost stopped to give her his own, but every time he slowed down, Charibert impatiently nudged him forward.

Despite Owun's curiosity about his sister's underground room, he'd offered to climb a tree at the edge of the overgrown field and keep watch. When they left him, he'd reluctantly given Father's sword back to Cloud. He was entranced by the blade. He could hardly stop looking at the crest. But if soldiers happened to come, a peasant perched in a tree with what was obviously a king's prized sword would look suspicious, to say the least. The four of them had decided on a warning signal — three shrill whistles in imitation of a bird call that Owun did well — if he saw anyone approaching.

Genofeva stopped, panting. She shielded her eyes against the sun's glare and studied the landscape around her. "I'm sure this is the area. There's a post sticking up somewhere behind some tall bushes. I remember it because I thought it probably once held the door. See if you can spot it."

They scanned the surroundings. She hadn't been joking when she'd described this place as spooky. Cloud found himself half hoping they wouldn't locate the hideout.

Right when it looked like his wish might come true, Charibert pointed to a barely visible pole several yards to the left. "That thing?"

"Yes! That's it!" Genofeva hiked up her dress and waded through the sea of dying grass. Bree was lost from view, but Cloud could hear her rustling beside her owner. When Genofeva reached the post, she grabbed a thick tangle of overgrown bushes with both hands and wrestled to pull it aside. "The room's under this."

The thought of hiding in an underground room in the middle of this creepy field made Cloud's mouth go dry.

Charibert joined Genofeva. "Here, let me do it."

She stepped out of his way and he started hacking the stubborn foliage with his sword.

"Careful," she said. "The stairs are really steep. Don't fall down."

"Cloud, come on. Help me."

A strange feeling — was it jealousy? — fluttered inside Cloud's chest. He didn't want Genofeva to think Charibert was more gallant than he. So he forced himself forward and knelt down next to his cousin, yanking back the thick undergrowth as

Charibert chopped away.

"I'm sorry," Genofeva apologized. "It wasn't this overgrown a couple years ago when I found it."

Charibert said, "That's good. It means no one has been here since."

Cloud desperately wanted to keep it that way. Who knew what was down there? Did bears hang around underground? Snakes did. There might be giant man-eating spiders. Or skeletons. Or a madman with an axe. The plea, *Can I please find somewhere else to hide?* almost tumbled out. But he bit the words back. He didn't want to look like a coward in front of a girl. Especially not a girl as pretty as Genofeva.

A few dismal minutes later, he and Charibert stared at an eerie hole opening up beneath the gnarl of roots and bushes. A final few whacks with the sword, and a set of crumbling stone steps came into view, descending into darkness. Cold air breathed out at them. Chills crawled up Cloud's arms.

Charibert let out a low whistle. "This is ancient." His eyes sparked with excitement, as if he and Cloud had stumbled upon the adventure of a lifetime. He seemed to forget for the moment about the murders and why they were gazing into this sinister hole in the first place. Cloud couldn't help think, ironically, that if Theodoald and Gunther were with them, the discovery might have been thrilling. Well, sort of. Cloud couldn't get the image of man-eating spiders and skeletons out of his head. But at least with his brothers, he would have felt braver.

"I can't believe no one's ever found this." A grin took over Charibert's whole face and he lowered himself onto the first step. When it held his weight, he descended a couple steps further. "I wish we had a lantern."

I wish we had a different hiding place.

Genofeva picked up Bree and cuddled her close. "What's down there?"

Charibert peered into the darkness. "It looks like the entrance to a dungeon or something."

Cloud's heart plunged to his stomach. *Did Charibert have to say that?*

His cousin continued. "There must have been a fortress here at one time."

"A fortress?" Cloud's voice came out embarrassingly squeaky. He cleared his throat. "That's impossible. Uncle Childebert rules all this land."

"No, I mean ages ago. Like centuries. My guess is the Romans built this."

Cloud's memory spun back to his history lessons with the monks. The Romans had occupied Gaul hundreds of years ago. Suddenly it hit him that all these boulders weren't just boulders. The three of them had been hiking across a field of stone ruins.

"Well, are you coming down, or are you just going to stand there?"

Genofeva shook her head emphatically and clasped Bree tighter. "Not me."

"Cloud? Come on." A slight echo reverberated Charibert's voice. He let out a laugh. "Don't tell me you're chicken."

Heat washed over Cloud's face. His mind raced, searching for a way to get out of this without proving his cousin right.

An amused snort sounded from below. "I'll protect you from the monsters. I promise."

A shrill bird call shattered the air. Two more followed in quick succession.

"It's Owun!" Genofeva's eyes widened with panic.

"Hurry!" All trace of teasing fled from Charibert's voice. "Get down here, quick!"

Cloud didn't need to be told twice. He grabbed Genofeva's hand and together they hurried into the earth's black belly.

Chapter Eight

Charibert halted so suddenly that Cloud slammed into his back. Genofeva, in turn, bumped into his. Bree whimpered in her arms.

"Wait. I better conceal the entrance." Charibert kept his voice a whisper. "Stay here."

Cloud nodded, even though it was too dark for Charibert to see him. Cloud hadn't counted the steps, but judging from the murky light filtering from above, they were about twenty feet underground. He had no idea how deep the stairwell went. And had no desire to find out.

He pressed against the cold wall so that Charibert could squeeze past him without tumbling off the narrow step. Genofeva did the same. Tiny bits of loose stone crumbled beneath Charibert's boots as he climbed upward. Dust particles floated in the dim light. Cloud pictured the whole staircase collapsing. Forget the snakes and spiders; now he was worried about being buried alive. Despite the chill, perspiration trickled down his back. He hoped the musty odor of dirt and mold would mask from Genofeva the smell of his sweat.

Trembling on the step above him, she clutched his arm with a death grip. He clenched the hilt of Father's sword so hard his hand hurt. They both stood frozen, listening to the scraping and shuffling above them as Charibert hauled the dead branches back over the entrance. The stairwell turned pitch black.

Charibert must have judged it was safer to stay where he was, on the steps just below the entrance, rather than venture back down in the dark. "Shh, don't move," he whispered, barely loud enough to be heard. "I can hear horses."

Soldiers. Had to be. Cloud held his breath. He suspected Genofeva held hers too. Bree's little body shivered in her arms, sandwiched between her and Cloud. Above them, Charibert was so silent that Cloud almost wondered if he was still there.

The minutes ticked by with agonizing slowness. Barely discernible voices and the clomping of distant hooves reverberated from the ground above. Cloud imagined Owun perched defenseless in the branches of a tree somewhere and prayed he was safe. *Please God, don't let the soldiers look up and spot him.*

After what felt like an eternity, the sounds in the field faded. Genofeva exhaled loudly and Cloud sensed some of the tension in her body draining. Still, she didn't dare let go of his arm. Charibert remained deathly quiet, no doubt straining his ears to figure out what was happening aboveground.

Finally, what must have been a full ten minutes later, a faint bird call, followed by two more, broke through the silence and Charibert said, "They're gone." He cleared the branches away from the entrance and dim sunlight flooded the stairwell.

Cloud released his breath and slumped against the wall with relief.

"Genofeva, come up here."

Charibert didn't have to say it twice. She shot up the stairs like a released arrow. Cloud wished he could do the same.

"Go get your brother. Show him where we are." Charibert turned to Cloud below. "We need to get a message to the castle at Lutece. Grandmere will know what to do."

At the thought of Grandmere Clothilde coming to the rescue, Cloud felt a glimmer of hope.

* * * * *

"Do you own a wagon?" Charibert sat plopped on the top step, Owun beside him. Cloud sat below, hugging himself, trying not to think of monsters and skeletons and spiders.

"No, my lord."

"A horse?"

Owun shook his head.

Charibert huffed with obvious frustration. "Don't you have *any* transportation to Lutece? It has to be you who goes. I'd do it if I could, but I can't. My absence would be noticed."

"Our father owns a mule," Genofeva piped up helpfully from where she knelt on the ground, Bree in her lap, a safe distance from the creepy stairwell. "You can take her, Owun."

Owun rolled his eyes at his sister. "Sure. Steal Pap's mule and vanish. It's that simple."

"But why not? You could sneak out at night. Pap wouldn't even realize that you — "

Owun cut her off. "Don't be dumb, Genofeva. I have no idea where Lutece is. It would take me days to find my way there and back."

Days. The thought of spending days holed up in these cold ancient ruins sent chills through Cloud.

Owun said, "Besides, how could a peasant like me hope to see the queen?"

"That part's easy. I can write a letter explaining everything to Grandmere. But if you don't know the way —" Charibert let the sentence trail hopelessly off. He rubbed his forehead with both hands. "Well, we have to think of something. And soon. I need to get back to Uncle Childebert's castle before anyone grows suspicious."

The idea of his cousin leaving stabbed Cloud with fresh dread.

For a moment, all of them sat thinking in gloomy silence. Cloud's stomach growled, reminding him that he hadn't eaten since yesterday morning. He prayed they could figure out a plan soon, so that hopefully Owun and Genofeva could sneak him some food from their hut.

Suddenly Genofeva jumped to her feet. "The priest, Father Burh! He'll help us; he's a saint! And he owns a horse. He can go to the queen." And before anyone could react, she bounded off with Bree, calling over her shoulder, "I'll go get him!"

Chapter Nine

Thank You, God, Cloud thought for the hundredth time, *for Genofeva.*

After she'd fetched Father Burh, the kindhearted priest who lived near a remote chapel in the woods, she had done even more to help: she'd insisted Cloud keep Bree for company. And for that, Cloud was grateful beyond words. The thought of spending a night here alone was terrible. At least the dog was another living creature. A nice one.

Cloud could tell that everyone felt awful leaving him by himself in the ruins. But they didn't have a choice. With so many soldiers hunting for Cloud, Charibert's absence — or even a couple peasant children missing in the area — would trigger suspicion. And the last thing Cloud wanted was to endanger their lives as well.

Owun had brought him a bowl of goat's milk and a handful of carrots, which Cloud hadn't eaten yet, and the priest — after hearing the whole horrifying story — had rushed back to his cottage for a woolen blanket and a crucifix, which he gave to Cloud with his blessing before leaving on his urgent mission to Grandmere's castle in Lutece. Charibert had punched Cloud in the arm, telling him to beware of the monsters prowling beneath the stairwell, then promised to bring a torch and more food as soon as he could manage to sneak out again. Unexpectedly, his eyes had misted and Cloud realized that, despite his cousin's bravado, Charibert was traumatized by the killings too. How could he not be? Theodoald had been his friend. And Charibert had seen the blood-drenched corpses, not only of Theodoald and Gunther, but Grandmere's murdered retinue as well.

When everyone had left, and silence settled over the field, Cloud's fears came back in full force. He hunkered against the wall just below the entrance to the stairwell, as close to open air as possible, ready to bolt if anything materialized on the stairs below. Bree romped around aboveground, blissfully unaffected by the atmosphere of dread. Cloud hoped she would bark if anyone came near, which would give him warning. But could such a tiny dog protect him from whatever evil might lurk below?

Why did Charibert have to mention monsters before he left?

A rumble from Cloud's stomach reminded him yet again that he hadn't eaten since yesterday. So while Bree played, he sat warily on the steps and took a few crunchy bites of carrot. His mouth was dry and his hands shook as he lifted the bowl of milk. Despite his complaining stomach, he could barely eat. Theodoald's agonized last moments replayed in his mind in a never-ending loop. That, and Gunther's screams. It seemed irreverent to sit here and have a meal, even if it was just tasteless vegetables and lukewarm milk. Guilt at having survived made his insides knot. Why him? Why did he alone escape when his brothers, along with Grandmere's entire retinue, were slain? He should be grateful, but part of him wished he'd died too. Now he was on the run, the only remaining heir of Father's kingdom of Orleans. He would be hunted by his uncles for the rest of his life. How could they allow him to be crowned king after what had happened in the castle? Their only choice was to find him and kill him too. And they would go to any lengths. Killing

Grandmere's retinue had proved that.

A terrible thought struck. What if they murdered Grandmere Clothilde too? Or Charibert for helping him?

Feeling suddenly ill, Cloud set the carrots on the step, fighting the urge to throw up. Fear and overwhelming sorrow crashed over him. He could no longer hold back the tears. The dam broke.

Please God, he begged, *please help me. Please let Grandmere come soon, and keep Charibert safe. Jesus, I need You. I'm really scared right now.*

He lowered his face in his hands, his body racked with sobs. He missed his brothers so much. He didn't want to spend the rest of his life hiding, waiting for the sword blow that must someday come. How could this whole nightmare be happening?

Bree must have sensed his anguish, for she stopped exploring and bounded onto the staircase and into his lap. For what must have been the next half hour, she sat with him, cuddling against him and licking him until his tears were finally spent.

The rest of the day passed agonizingly slow. He tried to pray. He tried again to eat. Neither worked. When daylight finally faded and a curtain of blinking stars stretched across the darkening sky, Cloud fought off rising panic. There was no way he planned to descend deeper underground than necessary to find a place to lie down, so he huddled in Father Burh's blanket against the wall on the third to top step, his senses on high alert. Clenching the priest's crucifix in one hand, and his sword in a death grip in the other, he strained his ears for any sound from either above or below. His muscles cramped from the tension.

After trotting up and down a few stairs, Bree sniffed the carrot Cloud offered her, declined it, and instead slurped up the last of the goat's milk. Then she curled up in his lap and promptly fell asleep, no doubt exhausted from the excitement of her day. Her furry white body rose and fell to the rhythm of her gentle snores. Together with the blanket and his ripped purple cloak, she kept Cloud warm.

Lucky Bree. To be able to just sleep, totally unaware of danger. Cloud knew that for himself sleep was out of the question. The thought of soldiers, the thought of what sinister things slunk below, the thought of tumbling down the stairs should he accidentally doze off, jumbled together and promised to keep him wide awake.

He braced himself for the longest night of his life.

Chapter Ten

Just how long would it take for Father Burh to bring Grandmere?

Cloud sighed with impatience for the millionth time. He stretched his legs in front of him and rolled his stiff neck and shoulders, trying unsuccessfully to find a more comfortable position on the unyielding cold stone. He'd been sitting on this same step all last night and all today. Exhausted from lack of sleep, weak from hunger, and his throat burning with thirst, he stared at the midday sun above the stairwell, wishing it would bring more warmth. Dust and twigs swirled around the entrance to the stairwell, the wind picking up. A cold breeze blew through his sweat-soaked tunic and he pulled the blanket closer. Dare he sneak aboveground for a walk to work out the kinks in his muscles? Maybe he could find a stream somewhere. Wash some of the dirt off himself and slake his thirst. Should he risk it?

He chewed his lip, weighing the danger. Charibert had made him promise he'd stay put. Soldiers would hunt him until he was found . . . and killed. The replay of Theodoald's last moments exploded again in Cloud's memory and he shuddered, hugging his arms around himself.

He decided to stay on the step.

The thought of Charibert brought another stab of worry. Had

his cousin somehow been discovered helping Cloud? Had they punished him? Maybe they'd locked him up somewhere, never to be seen again. That had happened to Cloud's own mother. After Father was slain in battle all those years ago, Uncle Clothaire had taken Mother captive, supposedly to be his new wife. But he already had several wives at the time, so Mother never really married him. She simply disappeared off the face of the earth. It was the only time Cloud had ever seen Grandmere Clothilde angry. The sins of Uncle Clothaire, her own child, devastated her. She told him to his face that if he didn't repent and return Mother, he would burn in Hell. Uncle Clothaire had laughed. The king was wicked, no doubt of that. But was he evil enough to throw Charibert in a dungeon as well? His very own son?

Cloud consoled himself with the thought that surely his uncles would demand Charibert show them where Cloud was hiding before punishing him. So maybe Charibert was perfectly safe at the castle, or even pretending to search for Cloud, and no one had any idea that he was in on all this. But if that was the case, why didn't he return with the promised torch?

And why hadn't Owun shown up with more food and water?

And Genofeva . . . when would she come to collect Bree?

Where on earth was everyone?

The possibility that both Owun and Genofeva were also dead had haunted Cloud all morning. Charibert wasn't the only one who had risked his life by helping Cloud. If his uncles' soldiers had found evidence of Cloud hiding in Owun and Genofeva's woodshed, who's to say they wouldn't —

Cloud's thoughts were interrupted by a man's voice carrying on the wind. He froze and strained to listen.

More distant words. Someone answered. Cloud couldn't make out anything they said. How close were they? The edge of the field?

Both hope and fear jumbled inside him. Hope that it might be

Grandmere's soldiers, fear that it would be his uncles' instead. He pulled Bree into his lap, desperately willing her to stay quiet, and cowered against the wall. Even if he could gather the courage to flee further down the creepy stairwell, it was too late now. Stumbling his way down in the dark might make too much noise, especially if he tripped.

He clenched his hand around the sword, heart hammering. *Let it be Grandmere's men. Please God, please God.*

"Careful. There are many rocks." This time, Cloud could make out the words.

"Watch your step here."

The men's voices grew louder as they tromped across the field. Cloud imagined them coming straight towards his hiding place. Stones clunked under boots. Voices murmured. Twigs snapped. A strange jingling noise, like a little bell, tinkled once or twice, as if someone had accidentally rung it. Cloud didn't dare breathe.

"Perhaps you should wait here. You might stumble. We'll bring him out."

Whoever they were, they knew exactly where Cloud was. Sweat trickled down his back. His pulse thudded in his ears. How many were there? He'd only discerned two different voices so far.

"No. I've come this far. I'm going all the way."

A woman's voice. Cloud recognized it!

He dumped a startled Bree off his lap, dropped the sword, and blasted aboveground. "Grandmere! Grandmere! You came!" Ignoring the three figures surrounding her, he flew the distance between them and barreled into her arms, almost knocking her down. The bell-like sound jingled wildly. "You came!"

She struggled for a second to regain her balance after their collision, then wrapped him tightly in her arms. "Cloud. Oh Cloud. Thank God you're safe!" Her voice cracked. She held him so hard he could barely breathe. He buried his face in the folds of her tattered cloak. The material was the color of mud and felt coarse, almost itchy, not like the soft, pretty cloaks she always wore. He didn't know why. He didn't care why. All that mattered was Grandmere was here and everything would be alright now.

After long minutes, he pulled back, setting off the soft tinkling noise again, and Grandmere released him. He gazed up into her face. A rough hood, the same ugly brown, covered her head. Her eyes were red. Fresh tears streaked her cheeks. She reached up with a trembling hand to wipe them away. Cloud was shocked by how old and fragile she looked — so different from two days ago. Not even to mention her peculiar clothes.

"My lady, we must hurry." A man with massive shoulders stepped beside her. He too was bundled in a ragged cloak and hood, heavily concealing his features, but Cloud spotted a graying beard peeking through. Cloud blinked and glanced around. The remaining two men moved in, all three garbed like the most destitute of peasants. Dangling from a rope around each person's waist, Grandmere's included, hung a small bell. *What on earth?*

Then Cloud spotted the bulge at two of the men's sides, bulky beneath their draping garments. He realized what they were: hidden swords.

The third man, the only one with no bulge, peeled back his hood. Cloud instantly recognized Father Burh. Working quickly, the priest untied his rope and bell, and flung off his tattered cloak to reveal his normal clothes. Before Cloud knew what was happening, Grandmere had taken off Cloud's dusty royal purple robe and handed it to the large soldier with the graying beard, who stuffed it into a sack. Father Burh tossed the ugly cloak – which he'd moments ago been wearing – around Cloud's shoulders, then disappeared down the stairwell, presumably to fetch the blanket, crucifix, and sword.

With shaking hands, Grandmere cinched the rope around Cloud's waist and attached the bell. Then she pulled up Cloud's hood, completing the disguise. At the blank look on his face, Grandmere forced a little smile. "No one will come near us," she said. "We're lepers."

Oh. That explained the bells.

"We don't have much time." The second soldier, younger than the other, took Cloud's arm and steered him away from the hiding place. "Let's go."

"Wait!" Cloud stopped in his tracks. "What about Bree?"

The soldier's eyebrows arched. "What?"

"The dog." Cloud wrestled his arm from the man's grip and searched the ground for a ball of white fluff.

Grandmere said, "What dog?"

"A little white one. She stayed with me. We can't just leave her here. She belongs to my friend."

The thought of Genofeva made his chest flutter. An emotion he didn't recognize stabbed him hard. He glanced around the field, as if by thinking about her hard enough she might materialize.

"She's right here." The priest's voice cut through the silence.

Genofeva was here! Relieved — and unexpectedly happy — Cloud whirled around. At least he could thank her and say goodbye. Maybe she and Owun would want to come visit him at Lutece. Would Grandmere allow that? Cloud couldn't think of a reason why not.

Father Burh smiled. "She was playing under the steps. What a cutie she is."

Oh. He meant Bree, not Genofeva. Cloud's heart plummeted. The dog squirmed in the priest's arms. He carried both the crucifix and sword. The blanket he'd lent Cloud lay draped over one shoulder. "Don't worry. I'll bring her back to Genofeva." He winked. "I can tell her parents I found her dog in an abandoned field. It's the truth, and they won't suspect a thing."

Cloud's brief surge of hope fizzled. So he wouldn't see Genofeva again after all. It was ridiculous that it bothered him. He'd known her hardly a day. She was a total stranger. Still, Cloud couldn't shake his disappointment.

The priest handed Cloud's sword to the bearded soldier, who secured it beneath his cloak. Bree wriggled free and bounded to Cloud. Dropping to one knee, he stroked her soft fur, a strange sorrow filling his heart at leaving her too. "Thanks for staying with me, Bree," he said. "I'll miss you. Take good care of Genofeva." He swallowed. "And Owun too." It wasn't just Genofeva that Cloud wanted to thank. He equally owed his life to Owun. And of course Charibert. But he'd see Charibert soon enough. Surely Grandmere would whisk away her other grandson and keep him safe at her fortress too. For all Cloud knew, Charibert was already at Lutece waiting for him. Being together with his cousin would be some consolation.

The priest bent next to Cloud and Bree and urged the crucifix into Cloud's hands. "Keep this, my brave prince. May God protect you." He made the Sign of the Cross over Cloud, then laid his hands on Cloud's head for a long moment.

The bearded soldier shifted and cleared his throat. "My lady, we really need to leave."

"Grimald is right, Cloud. We have to go." Grandmere gently pulled him to his feet. He reluctantly stood, thanked the good priest, and tucked the crucifix into the rope around his waist, next to the funny little bell. Father Burh would take care of everything here. As Cloud and Grandmere followed the man named Grimald, the younger soldier walked behind them, guarding their rear. Cloud searched for the horses that would take them back to the protection of Grandmere's castle, but he couldn't see any. The soldiers must have concealed them well in the trees beyond the field.

Grandmere slipped her frail hand into Cloud's as they trudged through the rocks. He clutched it tightly, partly to prevent her from stumbling, but mostly because he didn't want to leave her ever again. The shapeless tattered hood hid her face, but the droop of her head and her heavy steps revealed the deep grief that must weigh down her heart. Poor Grandmere. Cloud ached for her, almost forgetting his own sorrow. He couldn't even count the number of murders that had already stripped her so violently of those she loved. Theodoald and Gunther were only the most recent in the long line of bloodshed that had spanned Grandmere's life. Cloud had no doubt she loved his brothers as much as she loved him. What horror must she be feeling now, knowing they were slain by the sword of her own bloodthirsty son?

Was this the price of Grandmere's holiness? The way to sanctity? Relentless sorrow, united to that of her Crucified Lord?

Cloud suspected he knew the answer . . . and shuddered.

Chapter Eleven

To Cloud's amazement, the leper disguise worked. Twice as they tramped through the woods, they spotted soldiers in the distance. But at the mere ringing of the bells around their waists, the soldiers hightailed it in the opposite direction, scrambling to get as far away as possible from the foursome with the loathsome disease.

Cloud was equally amazed by Grandmere's endurance. They'd been trudging over the difficult terrain for what must have been half an hour, yet she'd kept up without complaint. Cloud suspected it was all the walking she did, visiting the poor in the countryside surrounding Lutece, that kept her fit. She always insisted on going on foot. She didn't want the peasants to see her as a grand lady in a fancy carriage.

Finally through the trees Cloud spied a cluster of four horses. It was only then that Grandmere released a sigh of relief, the first sign of her tiredness.

Grimald hurried ahead to the mounts and untied them. Then he carefully helped Grandmere onto the back of a bay mare that Cloud recognized as the gentlest horse from her castle stable. Cloud had never seen Grandmere ride, but he knew she could. He'd heard stories of her riding bravely with Grandpere Clovis as he traveled across Gaul with his army towards whatever battles he'd fought in those long-ago days. Whether those particular tales were true or not, Grandmere had once upon a time been a young princess who surely knew how to handle a horse. It was probably only her modesty and age that kept her out of a saddle now. How strange to think of Grandmere Clothilde having once been fiery and young and pretty.

Cloud wondered if she'd been like Genofeva.

He shook his head, annoyed at himself. Why was he still thinking of Genofeva? For heaven's sake, he'd only known her five seconds. She'd probably already moved on to her next adventure — Cloud was sure someone with a personality like hers had many — and forgotten all about him. What was a prince hiding in her woodshed amongst the many escapades she probably had? He suddenly wished he'd given her his purple cloak back in the field. He would have, if Charibert hadn't been in such a hurry. Cloud should have stopped and done it anyway. Maybe then Genofeva would remember him, if she had his cloak.

Or more likely, she'd be killed.

He shuddered and pulled his thoughts back to the horses. The younger soldier, who Cloud learned was named Rog, held the reins of a black gelding, gesturing for Cloud to mount. Cloud obeyed and hoisted himself onto the animal's back. Within moments, all four of them were mounted and riding as fast as they dared through the forest. Cloud forced himself to focus on the feel of the horse beneath him and not to think of everything that had happened since he'd fled Uncle Childebert's castle.

In less than ten minutes, a horrible thought struck.

What if Genofeva liked Charibert instead?

Charibert had been gallant. Had taken charge while Cloud just stood there like a dummy. Did girls find Charibert handsome? Huh. Cloud had no idea. Charibert was just Charibert. Was he good looking? Cloud squished up his eyebrows, trying to picture his cousin the way a girl might. He was tall and, come to think of it, his muscles kind of bulged beneath his — *Oh stop it.* Who cared if Genofeva liked Charibert! It wasn't as if either of them would ever see her again. Cloud definitely wouldn't. Charibert might, but it was unlikely. She was a peasant. They were both princes. Their worlds would never — *could* never — entwine.

Still, Cloud decided that when he met Charibert at Grandmere's castle, he'd sneakily try to find out if Charibert and Genofeva liked each other.

The thought of soon being reunited with Charibert sparked a tiny consolation. Cloud had never felt close to him, what with Theodoald always telling him to scram whenever their cousin showed up. Cloud and Gunther had been deemed too little to join in the big boys' fun. But now a life-and-death bond had been forged between Cloud and Uncle Clothaire's son, and Cloud found himself looking forward to being together at Lutece. Surely, after all that had happened, Grandmere would take her other grandson under her care now too!

With these thoughts running through his head, Cloud was surprised when Grimald, riding in the lead, pulled rein. The soldier's horse slowed from a lope, then lurched to a stop, setting his bell jingling with the abruptness. Grimald twisted in his saddle. "We're at the junction, my lady. This is where we part."

Grandmere and Rog halted, and Cloud reined in as well. He looked around, confused. He and Grandmere were parting from the soldiers? He frowned. That didn't sound safe. What if they got attacked on the way to Lutece? How could he defend Grandmere? Hopefully Grimald would at least give him his sword back. He swallowed, apprehension mounting.

Grandmere looked at him and her eyes filled with fresh tears. She tried to blink them away, but it didn't work. A trickle escaped down her cheek. It was awful to see Grandmere cry. Cloud wondered why she was crying again now. Surely things would be better soon.

She slipped off her horse and came over to him, reaching up towards him in an awkward embrace. Automatically he leaned down to hug her, wondering what was going on.

"Grimald will take good care of you, Cloud. Obey him and be a good boy." Grandmere's voice cracked. "I know you will."

What? Bewilderment made it impossible to speak. *Was . . . was he the one separating from Grandmere?*

She must have sensed his confusion. Her gentle eyes bore into his. "I know this is hard, Cloud. But you can't come with me. My castle is the first place my sons will look for you." She released him from their clumsy hug and dabbed at her teardrops. "Grimald is going to take you somewhere that no one will ever find you. You will be safe there. God will protect you, my dear Cloud. Stay close to Him and our Blessed Mother, no matter what happens." Her voice broke. "I love you."

Grandmere swayed slightly, as if overcome with emotion, then, her tears flowing freely, forced herself to return to her horse. Cloud sat in stunned silence as she remounted. Then he desperately called out, "Wait! I love you too! Please don't go!"

But it was too late. She gave him one last long loving look, then she and Rog rode away and disappeared into the gloomy woods.

"This way," Grimald said, turning his mount in the opposite direction.

"What . . . what's happening?"

"I'm taking you to Rheims."

Cloud had no idea why. All he knew was that his world, what little remained of it, had just collapsed.

Chapter Twelve

"My child, you must believe this. God loves each soul so perfectly, so intimately, that He sometimes flips the entire world upside down, just to prove that love."

Cloud lowered his eyes, too ashamed of his thoughts to hold the bishop's intense gaze. Indeed, God had completely flipped his world the last few days, but Cloud struggled to see any love. His brothers were dead; his own life lay in ruins. Everything he knew and treasured had been ripped from him in one horrible day. He was nothing now but a fugitive, hiding in a strange palace, on the run for the rest of his life. As he knelt before Bishop Remigius, feeling scared and oh so alone, it seemed impossible to find God's love in the destruction.

"I know, child. I know. You don't understand." The bishop's voice held sadness, but no reproach. He leaned forward in his velvet-cushioned chair and reached out, gently lifting Cloud's chin, urging him to raise his head. Reluctantly Cloud looked up. "But one day, you will." The old man's eyes sparkled with kindness. The purity and love shining from his face reminded Cloud strangely of Grandmere. People said the bishop of Rheims was a saint. Looking at him now, Cloud thought it must be true. "God loves you, Cloud. He loves you fiercely, with a love you can't even fathom. He allows these events only for a greater good."

Grimald impatiently touched Cloud's arm, a reminder of what he was meant to do. Cloud had never knelt in front of a bishop before; how was he supposed to remember to kiss his ring? But at the soldier's urging, he bent his head and offered the expected reverence. Satisfied, Grimald pulled him to his feet.

To Cloud's surprise, Bishop Remigius also rose, hoisting his frail frame with some difficulty out of the fancy chair. "Come. I will show you your room."

What? The prelate was going to take Cloud to the room himself, instead of summoning a servant? Cloud blinked, taken aback by such humility. But Bishop Remigius winked at him, as if they were old friends sharing a secret. "I hope you like the furnishings. Despite the short notice, I tried to decorate it for you." He chuckled and took Cloud's hand in his own. "I can't remember being a nine-year-old myself, so if you find anything too silly, just let me know." Then turning to Grimald, he said, "Please, my friend, help yourself to refreshments in my dining room. You know where it is, right?" He flapped a hand towards a corridor that looked awfully private. "Just through there."

Wondering if the soldier was as surprised by the invitation, Cloud left him behind and walked hand-in-hand with the saint — for he was sure now the rumors of Bishop Remigius's holiness were true. Imagine a bishop sending a soldier to raid his own table . . . and decorating a visitor's room by himself! Unheard of. Some of the pent-up tension in Cloud's muscles released. For the first time since he'd left Grandmere two days ago, he felt a measure of safety.

"How did you know I was coming?" he asked in a reverent whisper, not sure if he was allowed to talk out loud in an ecclesiastical palace, which, after all, belonged to the Church and was different from the palaces he'd grown up in.

"Your grandmother sent a messenger ahead, to tell me the tragic news and beg my help." Bishop Remigius halted and squeezed Cloud's hand. He looked down, his kind eyes drilling into Cloud. "I am so sorry about your brothers. I know you are much grieved. But they are safe with God. He loves them infinitely. Taking them now was the most perfect and loving thing He could do."

If anyone else had said something like that, Cloud would have been angry. How could someone tell him his brothers' brutal murders were an act of infinite love? But somehow, coming from Bishop Remigius, it sounded not only normal, but perfectly believable. Before Cloud could wrap his head around how the bishop could say such a thing and actually make it consoling, the prelate started walking again.

"We'll get you settled and fed, and let you rest. Sleep in as long as you need in the morning. In a few days, when you're feeling better, we can introduce you to your tutors and ease into a routine." He led the way up a sweeping staircase.

Tutors? Routine? Did this mean Cloud would be staying here for a while? Anxiety fluttered in his chest. "When can I go back to Grandmere's?"

The bishop stopped again, right in the middle of the stairs. This time he turned so that he could clasp both of Cloud's hands in his own. His grip was soft and warm and fatherly, more gentle than any touch Cloud could remember from his own father. But the saint's words knifed his heart.

"Never, my child. You will never go back."

Chapter Thirteen

Never.

The brutal word echoed through Cloud's mind, as it had for the past five days, tormenting him with its finality. The bishop had said he would never return to Grandmere, never go home.

Cloud stared out the window of his new bedchamber, more miserable than he'd ever been. Less than a week in Rheims and he already detested the sight of the bustling, noisy street below. An endless stream of peasants and peddlers, merchants and money-changers, beggars and braying donkeys paraded through the rutted road every hour of the day. All the sounds, strange smells, and commotion gave Cloud a headache. He longed for Lutece with its familiar country roads and wayside chapels. He yearned for his old surroundings, for the quiet woods which would be ablaze in autumn reds and oranges and golds. He would give anything to awake from this nightmare.

My child, God loves each soul so perfectly, so intimately, that He sometimes flips the entire world upside down, just to prove that love.

Every time Cloud thought the word *Never*, the bishop's other words strangely popped into his head too, as if Cloud's Guardian Angel was stubbornly pounding them into his skull. *God loves you. He loves you fiercely, with a love you can't even fathom. He allows these events only for a greater good.* Cloud could almost hear Bishop Remigius's voice in his ears, repeating the words endlessly. He didn't understand how good could come from any of this, much less *greater* good. But one thing Cloud did understand, and that was that he must be brave. No matter what. Princes were brave, always brave.

Not that Cloud felt like a prince anymore, clothed in this drab gray tunic with his hair bunched beneath a hood some servant had hastily sewn onto it. Grimald had wanted to cut his long locks, but Bishop Remigius insisted Cloud keep the unmistakable sign of his royalty. He must never forget he was still the rightful heir of Orleans, even if his identity, and thus his long hair, must remain concealed until — *until when?* Cloud didn't know. Maybe until he was eighteen and old enough to fight his uncles and claim his throne.

He shifted his gaze from the window to the bedchamber door. His new tutor was late. Usually by now he'd fetched Cloud for his morning lessons. It had quickly become apparent that Bishop Remigius had no intention of letting Cloud's education slip. Latin, history and rhetoric filled the morning hours, followed by lunch and a walk with the bishop in the palace gardens. Lunch and the walk were the only bearable moments of the day. Thinking of them actually made Cloud smile.

Yesterday Bishop Remigius had held Cloud spellbound with the story of Grandpere Clovis's miraculous victory on the battlefield of Tolbiac in the year 496, long before Cloud was born. Grandpere had been a pagan back then, much to Grandmere Clothilde's sorrow. Yet, greatly outnumbered by his enemy, a fierce Germanic tribe called the Alamanni, Grandpere had turned in desperation to the God of Grandmere Clothilde — the true God, of course — vowing that if he won the battle, he would accept Christianity. The tide turned dramatically, bringing a magnificent victory for Grandpere and his troops, and on the following Christmas Day, Bishop Remigius himself baptized not only Grandpere Clovis, but three thousand of his soldiers, right here in the Cathedral of Rheims.

The bishop was full of tales of Grandpere Clovis, but yesterday's was one of Cloud's favorites. He loved the story from the day before too, about a holy hermit named Severin who had miraculously cured Grandpere from an illness in his youth. Apparently the hermit was still alive, and a friend of the bishop. Imagine that!

It wasn't just the amazing stories the bishop told that filled Cloud with wonder; there was something about the man himself that was awe-inspiring. Cloud felt certain that if he'd been able to meet Jesus Christ on earth all those hundreds of years ago, the Savior would have acted like Bishop Remigius. Dining and strolling with the saint every day lifted a bit of Cloud's loneliness for that one precious lunchtime hour.

But following the short noon respite always came Cloud's most grueling lessons: weapons training, swordsmanship, learning the tactics of war. Five long, brutal hours he spent daily in the saddle, parrying against Grimald with wooden swords and spears until every muscle screamed in exhaustion. It wasn't at all like the play-fighting he'd enjoyed so much with Gunther. This was serious. And no matter how tired or bruised he was, no matter how many times Grimald unhorsed him and he crashed to the hard ground, the soldier never let up. *"You're a prince,"* he'd say. *"You must master these things if you intend to stay alive."* Never mind that Cloud was only nine years old; Grimald had no mercy. The sessions took place in a secluded field, not far from the bishop's palace, yet far enough away from the eyes of curious townspeople. Cloud already knew that when he grew up, he would have to meet his uncles in battle and claim his kingdom. The riding techniques and swordsmanship that he was learning now were life-and-death skills, without which Cloud stood no chance of success . . . or survival.

A few weeks ago, before God had done His thing and flipped the world, the thought of war had thrilled Cloud. How often he'd dreamed of riding into battle with a mighty sword. But now the prospect of the war he would have to fight and the uncles he'd have to face again, filled Cloud with icy dread.

On the busy street below, laughter erupted, interrupting his thoughts and jerking his attention back to the window. A cluster of adolescents had wandered into view. There must have been nearly twenty of them. Their shabby clothes and way-too-thin bodies definitely marked them as the city's poor, but their excited voices made Cloud's heart leap with unexpected longing. He eagerly leaned forward to watch. This was the first occasion he'd seen so many young people together at one time in the street since coming to Rheims. Memories flashed of his two brothers, and sadness swelled inside. He missed them so much. He hadn't been with anyone except adults ever since Charibert, Owun, and Genofeva left him in the dungeon stairwell. He missed all three of them too, with an intensity that surprised him. Especially Genofeva, for some dumb reason.

Everyone in the group below looked older than Cloud. Most were definitely in their teen years, with a few slightly younger. They chatted and jostled each other in a teasing, friendly way, as if they'd know each other for ages, until they reached a small house at the edge of Cloud's vision. Curiosity got the better of him and he stuck his head and upper body out the window to watch. The door opened and a woman, dressed in what looked like a black habit, stepped into the street. A long veil, covering her hair, rippled behind her in the gentle breeze. Immediately the group surrounded her. She smiled at them with words of greeting that Cloud couldn't catch.

Cloud tilted his head in wonder. The lady couldn't possibly be their mother; they were too old and there were too many of them. Yet whoever she was, it was obvious they had come to see her.

She started herding them into the house, which was more of a task than one would imagine, especially with so many teenage boys. They reminded Cloud of the way Theodoald and Charibert used to goof off. In the midst of the bustling, one boy happened to look up. He spotted Cloud leaning out the window. Cloud froze in alarm. Oh no! He wasn't allowed to be seen!

Before he could jerk his head back through the window, the other smiled and waved his hand towards the house and the lady in black. Whatever he thought of seeing a strange boy in the bishop's palace, his gesture was an unmistakable invitation to join them. Cloud sucked in a breath, not sure if he should wave back or withdraw and hide.

At last, the whole rambunctious group tumbled inside the house and the black-clad woman closed the door with what looked like a sigh of relief. The voices faded and the street returned to its usual noisy but depressing state. Cloud's shoulders slumped.

Part of him yearned to go with them. They were older, yes, but had all looked friendly, and right now he'd kill for a friend. And he was curious about the lady and what they were doing in her house. Whatever went on inside, it couldn't possibly be more boring than memorizing Latin declensions and listening to his tutor drone on about ancient history. He wondered if the group went to the lady's house every morning. Usually by now he was with his tutor, so for all he knew, they passed his window every day.

Cloud sighed. There was no hope he could join them. He was in strict hiding. He must remain invisible. Besides, he had all his tedious lessons to attend. Sudden loneliness overwhelmed him.

Then, just before he pulled his head back into the room, the door of the house unexpectedly reopened. The same boy poked his head out and looked up at the window. He waved insistently, again beckoning Cloud to come.

Chapter Fourteen

It was easy to slip out of the palace. The corridors remained empty and no one saw Cloud tiptoe down the stairs. He pushed back guilt at ditching his lessons and hoped the bishop would understand. After all, wasn't it rude to ignore an invitation — especially one given by a peasant? That's what Grandmere Clothilde would always say: *"We must serve the poor with special kindness, and never look down at them, but rather treat them as our masters."* She was always coming out with things like that. Cloud wasn't sure if this counted, but at least he could use her words as his excuse if he got in trouble.

By the time he wound his way through the busy street and reached the mysterious house, the boy who'd waved at him had disappeared. Cloud stopped at the door and hesitated. The place seemed strangely quiet. Had everyone departed while Cloud was sneaking out of his room? He had no idea. Should he knock, or simply walk in? As a prince, he'd rarely been in situations where he didn't know what to do. Sudden nervousness coiled his stomach. What if someone asked him why he was staying in the bishop's palace? Had anyone else noticed him in the window, besides that one boy? Could people tell he was royalty just by looking at him? For all Cloud knew, the story of his brothers' deaths and his escape from Paris had already spread throughout the land. Was everyone looking for a hidden prince? What if the woman in black recognized him and turned him in?

He swallowed.

No, he told himself, *how ridiculous*. How could she possibly know who he was? Even if news had spread as far as Rheims, why would she have reason to suspect he was the fleeing heir of Orleans?

Still undecided, he glanced down at his clothes. The gray tunic the bishop had given him was nondescript. The material was coarse, not at all like something a prince would wear. And his long hair, the only dead giveaway, was safely tucked beneath its hastily-attached hood.

Not quite sure why he was risking this, other than his longing for a friend, he sucked in his breath and tugged on the door. It opened with a soft squeak. The room was crammed, teens spilling into every nook and corner, their backs toward Cloud. A few perched on wooden benches, but most sat on the floor in front of the lady in the black habit, who was seated on a stool, facing slightly away from Cloud. Thankfully she didn't notice his entrance. He hesitated, then silently slipped inside, heart pounding. Despite the chilly air outside, the combination of so many bodies and the crackling fire made the room uncomfortably warm.

The lady was speaking while everyone listened. Cloud instantly recognized the story she was telling; Grandmere had told it many times to him and his brothers.

"And then Jesus answered the rich young man, telling him that if he *really* wanted to be perfect, he should sell all his possessions, give the money to the poor, and follow Him. If he was willing to do this, Our Lord promised him unbounded happiness and eternal life. In fact, he was being invited to be one of the Apostles."

"Which Apostle is he?" asked a girl on the floor.

The lady shook her head, as if to silence her. "You're getting ahead of the story. Does anyone know what happened? Can anyone tell us?"

A few murmurs. Faces turning to friends. Shrugs. Amazingly, no one seemed to know the story. Cloud couldn't believe they'd never heard it before.

"Tell us, Sister," someone finally said.

Sister? Cloud jerked with surprise. All these children were siblings? There were so many of them! Was that even possible?

"No one knows what happened?" The lady looked disappointed. "Not one of you?" She searched their faces.

Cloud couldn't help it. "I know."

Twenty startled gazes flew to the door. After a moment of surprise, the lady recovered and an impossibly beautiful smile creased her face. "Oh gracious, I didn't even see you standing there. Welcome. Come on in, please."

Everyone stared at Cloud. Heat burned his cheeks.

"See! I did spot someone in the window."

Cloud recognized the boy who'd waved to him, who now elbowed the nearest person with a smirk, as if to say, *Told you so.* Up close, his clothes were even more tattered than Cloud had originally thought. It looked like his tunic had never seen a washtub. In fact, all of the children were so poor that they made Owun and Genofeva look like nobility in comparison.

"Come in," the lady repeated. "I'm so glad you've joined us." She alone had tidy and clean clothes. Her smile lit up the room. "I'm Mena."

What a strange name. Cloud had never heard anything like it before. His bewilderment must have shown, because the lady explained with a little laugh, "It's Greek. That's where my people were originally from, so I have an unusual name."

"We just call her Sister," a girl said. "It's easier."

Another girl, who looked like the youngest in the room apart from Cloud, added, "Besides, she's like a big sister to us."

Well, at least that explained how she could have so many siblings. She didn't.

"Do people in Greece always dress in black?" The question popped out before Cloud could think.

"Oh heavens, no!"

"Then why do you?" Cloud was genuinely curious.

"I wear black as a symbol of having given myself to Christ." With that, she dismissed the subject with a joyful smile and little wave of her hand. "I'm so happy you're here. We meet nearly every day. You're always welcome to come."

The boy who had beckoned to Cloud at the window explained, "Sister teaches us about God."

Cloud wondered why their parents didn't teach them about God. Why did they need someone else? Huh. Maybe they were orphans. Judging by their poverty, that could easily be the case.

"What's your name?" the same boy asked.

"Cloud."

Giggles erupted among a few girls. A couple of the older boys nudged each other with amusement.

"What kind of fancy-pants name is that? And we thought Sister's name was unusual!"

Sudden horror knotted Cloud's stomach. He remembered, too late, that his name was not that of a commoner. To anyone who knew these things, his very name set him apart as royalty. Mere minutes ago he'd been worried that they might have heard of the escaped prince; now he'd given away his identity!

Sister Mena's eyes widened and something unreadable flashed across her face.

The hot room grew instantly hotter. Beads of moisture gathered on Cloud's neck beneath his warm hood.

Sister quickly recovered from whatever she was thinking and the serene smile returned to her face. "Welcome, Cloud." She bowed her head. It was a split-second gesture of respect that probably no one else saw, but Cloud caught it and knew what it meant. Sister had guessed his identity. She knew he was the missing prince. But when she next spoke, her voice gave nothing away. "Please, Cloud, have a seat." She smiled again, obviously trying to put him at ease.

Several of the students scooted over on the floor, making space for him. Not knowing what else to do, Cloud sank down between a teenage boy and the girl that looked the closest to his age. His heart galloped. Sweat trickled between his shoulders. Coming here had been a stupid idea.

Sister resumed the lesson as if everything was normal. She looked at Cloud. "So, you were saying a minute ago that you know what happened to the rich young man in the Gospel. Can you tell us?"

Cloud struggled to keep his voice casual. At least the story was short. "He didn't want to give up his money and his comfortable house. So he walked away."

A few skeptical eyebrows went up. One boy said, "You mean he's not one of the twelve Apostles?"

The girl next to Cloud gasped. "Really, Sister? Is that true? Someone actually walked away from Our Lord?"

"Yes. I'm afraid so. This one is a sad story. It broke Our Lord's Heart."

The boy at Cloud's side shook his head and murmured, "You'd have to be stinkin' selfish to choose land and riches over being an Apostle."

Another gave a derisive snort. "Rich people *are* stinkin' selfish. Haven't you noticed? Just look at our rulers. Name me one king or prince, *ever,* who cared about Jesus."

Cloud squirmed. A few minutes ago, he'd believed he blended in here, simply because he was wearing a boring gray tunic. But now, sitting with these destitute peasants on the floor, he was painfully aware of how their bones showed through their skin, and the stench of their threadbare clothes. His tunic, although drab, was perfectly clean and tidy. He was well fed and strong. Apart from the one day hiding in the field, he'd never missed a meal in his life. And worse, he was richer than anyone in this room could even begin to imagine.

By now sweat drenched his back. Strands of damp hair under his hood clumped against his neck.

Sister Mena came to his rescue. "That's a sweeping statement and not a fair one. Not all wealthy people are evil." She was rebuking the others, but probably only said it to comfort Cloud. She went on, "The rich young man in the story wasn't wicked. In fact, he wanted to be perfect, which is why he asked Jesus how. But, when it came down to it, he was too attached to his —"

She continued speaking but Cloud didn't catch any more of her words, because at that moment the girl next to him fanned herself and whispered, "It's so hot in here. How can you bear to have your head covered?"

Without warning, she reached over and tugged off Cloud's hood.

Chapter Fifteen

Cloud slowed his pace from a sprint to a staggering walk and fought to catch his breath. Ever since he'd fled Sister Mena's house, he'd been running blindly, with no thought but to get away. Everyone in the room had seen his hair tumble from his hood. Maybe no one else understood the significance of its length, but Sister Mena definitely did. Hardly a week in Rheims and he'd already blown his cover. He couldn't believe it. Why had he braved leaving the safety of the bishop's palace? *Stupid, stupid, stupid.*

He reached the edge of town, panting and sweating in his heavy tunic, wishing he could rip the ugly thing off. Stopping, he sucked in his breath and tried to calm his racing heart. With Rheims behind him, thick woods flanked his left, while to his right stretched fields and hills as far as he could see. A few scattered huts dotted the landscape. Thankfully, not a person in sight.

Relieved that no one had chased him, Cloud wiped the sweat from his forehead and tried to decide what to do. The obvious answer was to find his way back to the bishop's palace, admit what he'd done, and hope the bishop would find a way to fix this disaster. Maybe he'd bundle Cloud in a carriage and hustle him back to Grandmere's at Lutece. A tiny ball of hope throbbed in Cloud's heart. The thought of hiding in Rheims for the rest of his life was awful. Surely, the bishop would agree it was no longer safe to stay here . . . wouldn't he? After all, a roomful of people had just seen the unmistakable mark of his royalty.

Cloud glanced around, wondering if there was another way to return to the palace, rather than risk the road again. And that's when he spotted someone in a distant field. A man, garbed in some sort of robe with a small pack slung over his shoulder, was heading this way. He must have seen Cloud at the same time, for he raised a hand in a friendly wave.

To his horror, Cloud realized his head was still bare, his long hair exposed! In his panic to flee Sister Mena's house, he hadn't thought of jerking his hood back on. Had the traveler seen his hair? Cloud had to get away! The man was still at a good distance, but he'd be here within minutes. Cloud looked to the woods on his left. *Please Jesus, show me a place to hide!*

The second the prayer surged from his heart, he saw a little stone structure tucked amid the thick trees about thirty paces away. How had he not seen it before? Having no idea what the place was, he bolted towards it. *Please God, let that man go a different direction . . .*

The dwelling was tiny and primitive. A rotting wooden door hung partially open, but a curtain of cobwebs obscured what might be inside. Cloud swiped them away, yanked open the door, and ducked in. Musty, stale air immediately assaulted his nostrils.

The interior, barely large enough to hold four or five people, was strewn with cobwebs. Animal dung and weeds littered the dirt floor. Scraps of garbage, unrecognizable, lay smelly and discarded here and there on the ground, as if people had from time to time taken shelter here, perhaps during storms, then left without bothering to clean up. Near Cloud's feet sprawled a decaying rat carcass. The only other thing in the hut was a low stone shelf protruding from the wall opposite the door. Upon it lay a small figurine, toppled in a pile of mouse droppings and buried under what looked like years of dust.

Despite the state of neglect, an inexplicable aura of peace, mingled with intense sadness, permeated the room. *What was this place?* Curiosity replaced the fear of moments ago and Cloud stepped over to the shelf. He sensed that the toppled figurine was the reason for both the peace and the strange sadness that filled the tiny dwelling. He reached out and took the thing down, instinctively being gentle, to see what it was. At first he couldn't tell, so obscured was the object with dirt and sticky with cobwebs. It was only about a foot long, but surprisingly heavy, made of carved wood.

Using the hem of his tunic, Cloud rubbed away the surface grime. After a few minutes of cleaning, the resemblance of a person appeared. Parts of the wood had rotted away, but there was definitely a body, a face, and a round disk atop the head that unmistakably represented a halo. As soon as Cloud realized it was a statue, he knew immediately Who it was. It was Jesus. He was holding a statue of Christ, neglected and filthy and forgotten, in what Cloud now guessed was an abandoned wayside shrine.

Gazing at the statue, the sadness in the room seemed to penetrate Cloud's heart. How could anyone treat an image of Our Lord like this? The hut was too small to be a chapel, and the shelf was just that — a shelf and not an altar. But still, this place was holy. Someone, long ago, had piled stone upon stone, toiling to construct this little shrine. Someone had carved this statue with love and placed it here to be honored by wayfarers. It represented God Himself, He Who was worthy of infinite glory and devotion. Cloud remembered how reverently Grandmere Clothilde cleaned the religious images in her castle, how lovingly she arranged flowers in front of her beloved carving of Christ in her private oratory, how respectfully she bowed her head to the statues in the church. Yet the statue that Cloud held was caked with years of dirt, left lying upside down in a clump of mouse droppings, with nothing but trash tossed at His feet. Sorrow gripped Cloud, shocking him with its intensity. For a breathless moment it felt as if Jesus Himself stood invisibly in the room, heartbroken and lonely, pleading for someone to care.

"Are you lonely, Jesus? I know how you feel." Cloud swallowed. "I'm really lonely too." Then he did something he'd never done in his life: he impulsively hugged the statue. It was only a chunk of wood, but Cloud felt certain that the real Jesus was hugging him back. The sensation was so real that his body felt enveloped in a heavenly warmth, despite the chill of the shrine. For a few precious moments, everything else seemed to disappear.

He didn't know how long he stood there, invisibly clasped in his Savior's strong arms. It may have been mere minutes; it may have been longer. Time stopped. All Cloud was aware of was God's love pulsing through him and the anguish of Christ's rejected Heart beating against his own.

"Should we clean up?" A gentle voice sliced into Cloud's consciousness. "It won't take long if we do it together."

Startled, Cloud jerked back to the present, nearly dropping the statue. Disoriented, he spun around. A gray-haired man with a traveling pack stood in the doorway. It was the same man, the one in the long robe, who'd been walking through the field.

"I'm sorry. I didn't mean to startle you, my lord."

My lord? . . . What? Was the old man speaking to Jesus too?

Then the man gave a respectful bow and Cloud realized with shock that he himself was the one being addressed. His hood still hung down, his royal hair uncovered.

Chapter Sixteen

"My name is Severin." The man smiled, then added, as if Cloud might not remember, "I waved to you from the field."

Severin. The name sounded vaguely familiar, but Cloud couldn't place it. He swallowed, afraid of what might come next. Just like Sister Mena, this man obviously knew Cloud was a prince. But did he know *which* prince? The same dread Cloud had felt in Sister's house coiled again in his stomach. Would this be his reaction for the rest of his life — panicking every time his identity might be known?

But to his relief — and surprise — Severin didn't ask questions. In fact, he didn't even seem to expect Cloud to introduce himself. The old man merely glanced around the shrine and said, "What a sorry state this place is in. Shall we tidy up? Make it worthy again for our gracious King? What do you say?" He looked back at Cloud and his eyes twinkled with gentle mischief. He obviously wasn't talking about either earthly king. Uncle Clothaire and Uncle Childebert were anything but gracious! He was talking about Jesus Christ, the King of kings. Cloud sensed it was Severin's way of letting him know that he was safe here; that Severin guessed exactly who he was but wouldn't turn him in to his uncles. As if to confirm it, Severin reached over and carefully pulled Cloud's hood back over his hair. "I didn't see this," he said with a wink.

"I . . . I would love to help you clean the shrine." Cloud realized he was still pressing the statue against his heart. Embarrassed, he set it back on the shelf. But not before brushing away the mouse droppings.

Severin stepped back outside and with infinite care placed his small traveling pack on the grass next to the shrine door. He handled it so tenderly that Cloud couldn't help but ask, "What's in there that's so special?"

"My chalice."

"You're a priest?'

"I am. By the grace and mercy of God."

That explained his long robe.

"But why do you carry your chalice around? Shouldn't it stay in your church?" Cloud had never heard of a priest strolling around with a sacred vessel.

"I have no church. I'm a hermit."

"You mean you don't live anywhere?"

Amusement lit up the priest's eyes. "I live everywhere." He waved a thin hand, indicating the surrounding countryside. "The good God has given me all this. Everywhere is my home."

Cloud tried to imagine what it would be like to wander the land, going wherever you wanted. It didn't sound too bad. "But what do you eat? I mean, who feeds you?"

Severin's eyebrows rose, as if the question surprised him. "Why, God feeds me. He always provides. I have never gone hungry a day in my life."

"Oh." Cloud thought about it for a second and was almost tempted to ask Severin if he could join him. Anything would be better than holing up in the bishop's palace for the next ten years. But before he got the chance, Severin added, "Although these days my old legs complain from time to time. And I don't handle the cold like I used to. So when winter comes, I'm forced to hibernate in a little cave outside Paris."

Cloud instantly changed his mind. Not only did living in a cave sound awful, but Paris was Uncle Childebert's territory. The place of his brothers' murders. Cloud shuddered. He never wanted to set foot near Paris again. The urge to join Severin vanished.

As if reading his thoughts, the priest patted Cloud's shoulder. "Paris is far away," he assured in a low voice, even though no one else was around. "You are safe here, my lord."

There it was again. Severin calling him 'my lord.'

He definitely knows who I am, Cloud thought. *How could he not, coming from Paris?*

Changing the subject, Severin rubbed his hands together with enthusiasm and craned his neck back into the shrine. "What do you say, my young friend? Shall we get busy and clean house for the King?"

* * * * *

By the time they were done, Cloud's tunic was filthy and his stomach was ready for lunch. But he'd never felt so happy in his life. Pride at their accomplishment swelled in his heart, but it was more than that. During the whole time they cleaned, Cloud felt a breathtaking other-worldly presence, as if Jesus was right there, watching them work. Watching with love. And gratitude. Cloud had never thought about Christ being grateful before. He was God, after all. How could He be grateful for anything, when everything came from Him anyhow? But He *was* grateful. Cloud somehow understood that now.

Between the two of them, it had taken just over an hour. Cloud had constructed a broom from tree branches and swept the floor, while Severin dusted and scrubbed. Together they'd straightened the crumbling stones as best as they could and even managed to find a few handfuls of autumn wildflowers, which

82

the priest lovingly arranged around the statue on the shelf. Then they fixed the door and weeded the surrounding area. Cloud even lined a little path with pebbles leading to the shrine, with the hope that now travelers would notice it.

Earlier, as they'd worked, Severin had told Cloud he was friends with Bishop Remigius. In fact, he'd come to Rheims to visit him. Cloud had been too busy to make the connection.

But now, as they prepared to leave, it suddenly dawned on him. This must be the Severin of the bishop's story, the one who'd miraculously healed Grandpere Clovis! Holiness radiated from Severin the same way it did from the bishop. Imagine that! Meeting two saints in less than a week! And one of them worked miracles!

As Cloud stared at the holy man in newly found awe, he suddenly wondered if saints bunched together, kind of like bandits did. A gang of saints, power in numbers. A silly picture formed in his mind of a holy gang, Bishop Remigius and Severin among them. Clad in glowing armor with lily-white swords, they charged into battle with halos circling their heads. Cloud imagined Grandmere Clothilde appearing out of nowhere, a member of *The Gang*. In his mind, there were lots of them, holy men and women, whipping glowing blades and cutting down shrieking demons on the right and left. He almost laughed out loud at the ridiculous thought.

Yet it wasn't *too* ridiculous, was it? Grandmere was always telling him that spiritual warfare existed, and it was much more real and heroic and urgent than the blood-drenched battlefields Grandpere Clovis and his brave warriors had ridden upon. Countless times she'd told him that the most valiant soldiers — the only ones who *really* counted — were those who lived and fought and died for God's kingdom, not man's. She'd also complained, with great sadness, that Christ's army was abysmally small, tiny compared with the army of those who fought for worldly gain.

These thoughts spun through Cloud's mind as Severin gathered up his pack with his precious chalice. On impulse, Cloud went back inside the shrine and knelt to pray. His head swirled with images of battles and God's army, and he felt suddenly so blessed to have met three living saints. How many people could claim *that*?

As he looked up at the statue of Jesus, the one that had mysteriously *hugged him*, an invisible flaming arrow suddenly shot out from the statue and slammed through Cloud's heart, so real he gasped in pain. He reeled in agony, and clutching his chest, nearly lost his balance on the floor. Then the pain exploded into unspeakable bliss and longing, till he felt he would die of joy.

When the incredible feeling subsided, Cloud knelt there, dizzy and blinking, trying to figure out what Jesus had just done. It slowly dawned on him that God had wounded him with an arrow of love.

'God loves you, Cloud. He loves you fiercely, with a love you can't even fathom.'

Bishop Remigius's words.

And suddenly Cloud understood.

An overwhelming desire gripped him. All he wanted, with his whole being, was to serve the only true King.

Severin poked his head back inside, the precious pack with his chalice slung over his shoulder. "Are you ready to leave?"

Not trusting himself to speak, Cloud nodded and shakily stood up.

As they walked together to the bishop's palace, Cloud knew everything had changed. Outwardly, he'd merely helped an old man clean a wayside shrine. And he was still doomed to ten years of boring lessons and grueling horseback sessions and never having a friend to play with. He would still spend his days in hiding and loneliness, sweating under a hot heavy hood. But something, deep down, had radically shifted. Between a toppled statue, a kindhearted hermit, and an arrow wound, Cloud now understood the only thing that mattered.

To somehow join *The Gang*.

Nine Years Later

Chapter Seventeen

Cloud's muscles tensed as he reached the top of the hill and saw the first buildings of the city. Dread squeezed his lungs and he halted, his feet suddenly frozen on the path. It was almost impossible that his uncles would recognize him after nearly a decade, especially with Cloud wearing this long black cloak. But still, seeing Paris sprawled out before him chilled him to the core. He knew, from Bishop Remigius, that both uncles still wanted him dead. From where he stood, he could see Uncle Childebert's castle, squatting in the distance like some evil gray monster, drooling to devour him if he ever got too close to its jaw-like gates. His brothers had met death within those cruel walls. For all Cloud knew, their blood still stained the floor stones. He shuddered and tugged the heavy hood tighter around his head, feeling vulnerable with his long hair.

Maybe he should have finally cut it before coming to find Severin. So many times in the past nine years he'd wanted to chop it off, wanted to rid himself of the unmistakable sign of his royal identity, so he could make friends and go outside freely, without having to slink around in fear. But Bishop Remigius refused to let him cut it. Grandmere Clothilde, who kept in touch with the bishop — although she never dared come to Rheims for fear of bringing suspicion to Cloud's hiding place — had begged the bishop to keep Cloud's hair long.

Bishop Remigius was dead now, God rest his saintly soul, but Grandmere was still alive, and Cloud couldn't bring himself to disappoint her by disregarding her wishes. Her reasons, after all, were logical. Grandmere knew exactly what Cloud's future would hold. Or was *supposed* to hold, at least. All the years of warfare training in Rheims had been a preparation for one thing only. The kingdom of Orleans belonged to Cloud. He was its rightful heir, not Uncle Clothaire or Uncle Childebert, who had stolen it by treachery and murder. Cloud's princely hair, together with the giant sword at his side and his muscles hardened like steel — thanks to nine ruthless years under Grimald — were the three things that would bring him to his throne.

Only problem was, Cloud didn't want it anymore.

After Remigius died, Cloud was tempted to send a message to Grandmere that he wouldn't go to war. He didn't plan to kill anyone. He never wanted to wade through a battlefield knee-deep in blood, his sword stained and dripping with someone's insides. Who would choose that? Christ wouldn't. Saints didn't. *The Gang* didn't. He was eighteen years old now; he could choose his own future, couldn't he?

He sighed, unsure of the answer. Seared into his memory were the last words Gunther and Theodoald had ever heard Grandmere speak. As they climbed into the carriage on that fatal day, Grandmere hugged Cloud and his brothers, whispering, *"My children, I shall not think that I have lost my son, your father, if I live to see you reign from his throne."* Then, with those parting words from the person they loved more than anyone, they trundled off — Theodoald and Gunther to a gruesome death, and Cloud into a decade of exile. His brothers could never fulfill Grandmere's wish. But Cloud could.

So here he was, staring at the castle of his nightmares, his long hair still crammed beneath a sweltering hood in the blazing Parisian sun.

Before setting off on his journey, he'd sent Grimald to Lutece with a vague message for dear Grandmere that he was heading to Paris. She'd at least know where he was, and she could believe whatever she wanted to believe. In the meantime, Cloud would ask Severin for counsel. If, that is, he could find the holy hermit's cave. Severin had told him that he wintered in Paris. Well, it definitely wasn't winter, but maybe the priest would still be here. He was very elderly now, and doubtless frail. He'd stopped visiting Bishop Remigius a couple years ago. Cloud hoped that Severin was still alive, and that his dwelling could be found.

He'd have to talk to people and ask around. There was no way out of it, unless he was prepared to wander the outskirts of the city for days on end, poking his head into every cave and crevice. The priest's reputation for sanctity stretched far and wide, so surely his own people of Paris would know where he lived. Cloud intended to stay as far away from Uncle Childebert's castle as possible, which meant he'd limit himself to the areas where the poor dwelt.

But before hitting the streets and talking to anyone, Cloud first must see his brothers.

He instinctively tightened his hand around the hilt of Father's sword, and headed down the path.

Chapter Eighteen

Thankfully, the crypt of the cathedral was empty. Cloud didn't want anyone to see the emotion that overwhelmed him as he knelt at the tombs of Theodoald and Gunther. He suspected seeing their graves would be difficult, but the rawness of his sorrow surprised him. A dam inside broke, a dam he didn't even realize was there. Memories of their murders and the grief of loss slammed through him with the force of a tidal wave. Suddenly, violently, he missed them with every fiber of his being. His eyes stung hot and a tear slid down his cheek. Sadness threatened to choke him.

He swiped away the tear and traced his fingers gently over their names on the stones. Grandmere had brought them here to her favorite cathedral, the one she had begged Grandpere Clovis to build in honor of Saints Peter and Paul. Cloud was touched to see that the tombs of his brothers were fit for kings, every bit as ornate and costly as Grandpere's own, not far away in this same crypt. Cloud had visited the cathedral many times as a child. Every time, in fact, that he went to Paris with Grandmere. She'd always stop and kneel a long time at her husband's burial place, praying for the repose of his soul. Theodoald and Gunther were usually with them too, and all three would quickly grow bored with Grandmere's extended prayers and wander around the dimly lit crypt. Theodoald inevitably tried to scare Cloud and Gunther with spooky stories about graves cracking open and dead bodies springing out, until eventually their whispered voices became too loud and Grandmere would sigh and stand up and herd them back outside, sternly reminding them to behave in church.

Never once did Cloud imagine he'd be kneeling in the same crypt at the graves of his brothers.

They would have been in their twenties now. They would have been kings. Cloud himself would be a king, all three reigning over Father's divided lands. The thought was almost incomprehensible, so far removed from reality that it seemed ludicrous.

What would his brothers be like if they were alive? Surely they'd be just and kind. Compassionate to the poor, merciful to the suffering. They'd probably still tease Cloud; they always had. The baby brother, destined to be forever the pest. But they would love him, and the three of them would rule with peace. He couldn't imagine Gunther or Theodoald being selfish and violent like Uncle Clothaire. Like Uncle Childebert. Like . . . like —

Cloud winced. Like Father. Their own father.

Cloud's insides squirmed. He barely remembered either of his parents. He didn't even know if Mother was alive. But he wasn't ignorant about Father. Everyone knew the murders King Clodomir had committed, the people he'd tortured, the sinfulness of his life.

A second tear trailed down Cloud's cheek and he suddenly remembered Bishop Remigius's words, that God had allowed his brothers' deaths only for a greater good. Cloud hadn't understood it at the time, but now he did. Theodoald and Gunther had been spared the powerful temptations that kings faced. In God's infinite foreknowledge and mercy, He'd prevented them from growing up and being crowned. Kingship was a dangerous thing. A very dangerous thing indeed.

As for himself, Cloud wanted nothing to do with ruling a kingdom. But, as with his brothers, it would be God, not man, who had the final say.

Chapter Nineteen

"Excuse me," Cloud called out, approaching two men unloading a mule cart across the road. "I wonder if either of you can help me."

Both men looked in their mid-twenties. They were lifting heavy sacks of grain from the back of the cart, tossing them into a pile at the door of a rickety building. No one else was in sight, so it seemed a safe place to start asking about Severin.

Only one worker glanced over at the sound of Cloud's voice. He was dressed strangely, wearing what looked to Cloud like a toga, the kind of thing a Roman would wear. Then again, who was Cloud to talk about strange clothes? Here he stood in a long black cloak, his face obscured by its hood, in the blazing noon sun.

The second man, clad in normal peasant clothes, was too absorbed in a drama with a leaking sack to bother with Cloud.

"What do you need?" the one in the toga growled. Despite his flashy foreign clothes, the fellow couldn't be too important, doing work like that.

"I'm trying to find an old friend."

The Roman's sigh was so huge Cloud could hear it ten feet away.

"Hang on a minute." The impatient tone left no doubt that

helping Cloud was a burden. The man dumped the sack he was holding back onto the floor of the cart and hopped down. As he swaggered towards Cloud, he mopped his glistening forehead. His features were foreign, his expression anything but friendly.

Cloud adjusted his hood, making sure no strands of hair hung visible. Covering his head in this hot weather was clearly insane. Would the fellow be suspicious?

But the Roman — if indeed he came from Rome — wasn't looking at Cloud's hood. He'd noticed the sword, visible under the heavy black cloak. How could he not? The thing was huge. Inwardly, Cloud winced. Here he was, scrupulously careful to hide his hair, yet he'd been so unnerved entering Paris that he'd forgotten to conceal the sword. Being in Uncle Childebert's territory, he'd wanted the blade easily accessible, ready to draw in the space of a heartbeat should he run into danger. But normal folks didn't carry weapons. And certainly not massive, ornate swords of costly steel and impeccable craftsmanship. Only a man of great power and wealth owned a sword like this. No wonder the man stared.

The sight of the weapon darkened the man's already dark expression. He reached Cloud, planted his feet in a wide stance, and crossed his arms. The silent message of hostility could not be more clear.

"Whom are you looking for?" His words held both an accent and a dare.

It was too late to hide the sword, so Cloud kept his voice friendly and said, "There's a priest who lives in a cave somewhere around here. His name is Severin. Any chance you know him?"

"You mean the hermit?"

"Yes."

The man glared. "I know of him." He clipped the words.

After an awkward silence, it became obvious that no more

information was on the way.

"Mind telling me where he lives?"

"In fact, I do mind." The man arched his black eyebrows, then indicated the sword. "Strangers with weapons like that aren't welcome here."

Whether this Roman was someone of importance or not, he sure acted like he owned the place. He wasn't even a Frank. What nerve.

"Who are you? And what do you want Severin for?"

The temperature of Cloud's blood rose a few notches and a rude reply zipped through his mind. But he was trying hard to be part of *The Gang*, so no curt replies from him. Ignoring the question about his identity, he said, "Severin's my friend."

The other's eyes narrowed. Hostility oozed from every pore. "Oh really?" The way he said it implied that the priest couldn't possibly have affection for someone draped head to toe in black and so well armed. "Well, you're out of luck. He no longer lives in a cave. And if you were truly his friend, you'd know that. Now get lost." With a smirk, he turned to walk away.

"No, wait. I came from —" Cloud almost said *Rheims*, but caught himself. "I've come from a long distance. I really need to find him."

The Roman swiveled and studied Cloud's face. Maybe he could see the genuineness in Cloud's eyes because after a long moment he sighed and called out, "Hey, Owun! Come here!"

Owun?

For an instant, Cloud's heart stuttered. No, surely it couldn't be. There must be dozens of Owuns who lived near Paris. The name was common enough. What were the chances of running into the same Owun all these years later? Nonetheless, he searched for something recognizable about him. From this angle, it was hard to tell. Cloud hadn't seen him in nine years. Even if that was him — which was highly unlikely — how would Cloud know?

This particular Owun had climbed out of the cart by now. He was grabbing handfuls of spilled grain from the ground and impatiently shoveling them back into the ripped sack. He didn't bother looking up. "No, *you* come here, Tarquin! Help me get this cleaned up! Hegbert will kill me if we don't collect all this stuff."

Tarquin was a Roman name. Cloud's guess was correct.

Tarquin snorted with amusement and his mood seemed to lift, as if he found his companion's difficulty entertaining. Something like a grin spread across his face and he told Cloud, "I'll go ask him. Wait here." Despite the lighter tone, it still sounded like a command.

Tarquin strutted back to the cart.

Cloud watched as *maybe-Owun-maybe-not-Owun* huffed, then grudgingly stopped to talk with Tarquin. They kept their voices low. Tarquin pointed at Cloud's sword and the other fellow looked over. Tarquin's attitude made Cloud feel like a criminal. The black cloak and weapon made him *look* like a criminal. Should he leave? Just walk away? Or would that make him more suspicious? What if this Tarquin-fellow reported him to Uncle Childebert's soldiers? Would a foreigner bother to do that?

After a minute, *maybe-Owun* strolled towards Cloud. Tarquin followed, his arms once again crossed. Cloud could tell he was there for backup, should backup be needed.

This had been a bad idea, coming to Paris with the sword of King Clovis dangling for all the world to see.

The one named Owun reached him. "I hear you're looking for Severin the priest." He sounded uncertain.

"Yes. He's a friend of mine."

Like Tarquin had done, he stared at Cloud's weapon. "So, why do you want to see him?"

Good grief. Cloud pushed down annoyance at being interrogated by these two. If only they knew they spoke to a prince.

While the other's gaze locked on the sword, Cloud searched his face for anything recognizable. It *could* be the real Owun. He was obviously older, but the general build and hair color seemed what Cloud remembered. Cloud had met Owun so fleetingly, and he'd spent most of that day memorizing Genofeva's sweet face, not studying her brother's. It was hard to know.

"That's a mightily impressive weapon you have."

Well, Cloud decided, there was one way to find out if this was *his* Owun. It was risky, but Cloud had already drawn suspicion, so what the heck?

"Want to see it up close?"

Startled, the peasant stepped back in alarm. Perhaps he thought Cloud was threatening to draw the weapon against him. Cloud slid it from his belt. Tarquin jumped, his bravado vanishing. He looked ready to run.

"Here, go ahead and hold it."

After a long moment of hesitation, *maybe-Owun* reached out and accepted the sword. Cloud watched him carefully, waiting for his reaction.

It didn't take long.

His eyes widened when he saw the crest engraved on the blade. He blinked, then squinted, then stared at it, stunned.

Yep, he recognized it. He'd been in such awe of it nine years ago. He'd carried it — King Clovis's legendary sword — with such beaming pride and an air of disbelief as they'd hurried through the woods looking for Genofeva's hiding place. He'd been so disappointed to give it back to Charibert when he climbed into that tree as a watchman. It was probably the only sword he'd ever held in his life. He remembered it, no doubt at all.

His eyes flew to Cloud's face with confusion. As the significance of the black cloak and heavy hood dawned on him, his jaw dropped.

"Cloud?"

In a heartbeat, Owun crashed to one knee and loudly blurted, "My lord prince! I. . . I can't believe it's you! You're alive! And back in Paris!"

Horrified, Cloud swiftly reached out and jerked Owun to his feet. *"Shhhh!"* he begged. But it was too late. Tarquin had seen. And heard.

Had anyone else? Cloud frantically searched the road for others who may have witnessed the act of homage or heard Owun blare his name.

Not far away four women with woven baskets stood chatting outside a doorway. They hadn't been there a few minutes ago. One was staring this way. By the way her mouth gaped open, she'd definitely seen Owun thunk to one knee. She'd probably even caught Owun's loud words.

A line of sweat trickled down Cloud's back.

Recovering, Tarquin stormed closer, his eyes bugging out of their sockets. He looked at Owun, then at Cloud, then back at Owun. "Who is this?" he demanded. "And why in heavens did you kneel to him?"

Down the road, the woman elbowed one of her companions, and pointed at Cloud. She said something and the whole group stopped chatting. All four turned to stare.

"Who on earth *are* you?" Tarquin demanded again.

Before Cloud could think of a reply, Tarquin reached over and yanked off his hood.

So much for staying hidden. By nightfall, every tongue in Paris would go wild.

Chapter Twenty

Still amazed that he'd remained undiscovered for nearly three weeks, Cloud shoved the hammer into his belt, slapped the dirt off his hands and stepped back with pride to admire the first house he'd ever built. Admittedly the word *house* required a huge stretch of imagination, but it had four somewhat stable walls, a roof, and only leaned a little. But with the ground so marshy beneath it, what else could one expect? Hopefully the tiny dwelling would remain standing. Severin's hut, a few stones' throw away, was even more slapdash than Cloud's, and it had survived thus far without toppling. So Cloud hoped for the best.

"What do you think?" He grinned and turned to the priest.

"A castle fit for a prince." Severin smiled back. Then he frowned and pointed a frail finger at one of the corners. "It's sinking there, you know."

"That's your fault. You're the one who decided to live in a swamp, after all."

Severin raised both hands in surrender. "Not me. Blame Saint Clement."

He was talking about the nearby ancient chapel dedicated to the saint. Whoever chose to construct a church in a mud pool all those years ago must have been crazy. But the isolation of the area was perfect. No one ever visited the chapel. Probably hardly anyone knew of its existence. And thankfully no one had yet had the brilliant idea to search for the rumored mysterious prince in this forsaken marshland in the middle of nowhere.

"Owun will be disappointed," Severin said, "that you finished building your mansion without him. I think he rather enjoyed being in on the secret project."

"Well, I can always set him to work with a garden. Heaven only knows how to grow food in all this mud. Maybe Owun will have some hints."

The hermit clicked his tongue with mock disapproval. "How many times do I have to tell you, Cloud, that God provides? I've been here for years now and never once have gone hungry."

"Yes, well. I'm still going to try a garden." Cloud had no intention of any risky trips into Paris. Not after being seen by that group of women. Owun had confirmed that gossip was rampant, making staying out of sight a must. Apart from a food supply, Cloud had everything here he wanted. The Blessed Sacrament so close, a personal priest who offered daily Mass at Saint Clement's Chapel, and now a home to call his own so he didn't have to squeeze in with Severin anymore. Food was the only problem.

Food, and staying hidden. *That* was the tricky one.

With a twinkle in his eyes, Severin shook his snowy-white head. "Plant your little garden if you must."

"Rather, if I *can*."

"My friends always leave enough food." He said *leave*, rather than *bring*, because no one wanted to trek through the swampland with a loaf of bread for the holy hermit. People left things for him near the well at the edge of town, where Severin walked daily. Everyone loved the gentle priest; no one would dream of stealing the daily gifts of food. He'd been sharing it with Cloud for the last few weeks, but Cloud worried that the old man had too little to eat now.

"I'll ask Owun tonight if he knows anything about gardening," Cloud said. "I bet he does."

Owun had been sneaking up in the evenings when his work in town was done. He'd been a huge help in building the hut, bringing tools and wood, and even making a gravel path so that Cloud didn't have to slide in the mud every time he returned from Saint Clement's Chapel.

Countless times these last three weeks Cloud had almost asked him about Genofeva. Was she still living at home? What was she doing? Did she remember him? Did she even know he was here? Was she . . . *was she married?* Cloud always stopped himself in time before asking Owun anything about her. He wasn't sure he wanted to know. Especially the part about being married.

It irked him that he even cared. So what if the girl was married? So what if she'd forgotten his existence? She was a peasant, he was a prince, and they'd known each other for less than two days. Wondering about her life was a waste of time.

Besides, Cloud had given his heart wholly to God. Ever since that breathtaking moment of grace in the wayside shrine nine years ago, Cloud knew he'd never take a wife. He wanted to belong to God alone. He'd fallen into a routine since settling here in the marsh that he hoped to never break. Mass, work, prayer. He'd never felt so peaceful as he did in this quiet area with Severin.

Unlike Bishop Remigius, Severin had no problem with Cloud quitting the world to serve God. When Cloud asked him if he should cut his royal hair, the hermit had smiled and gently said, "I see nothing wrong with that. Only wait a bit longer, to make sure it's truly what God wants." Cutting his hair would be abdicating his royalty. He must be certain it was God's will, not his own.

Cloud hadn't told anyone, not even Severin, but in the

deepest recesses of his heart, a desire was growing. Cloud wanted to be a priest. Could that dream ever come true? A prince being ordained seemed even less likely than Genofeva falling in love with him. And *that* was very unlikely indeed!

Despite his secret longing for the priesthood, Cloud still didn't want to learn from Owun that his sister was married, so he never worked up the courage to mention her. Owun didn't bring her up either, which, strangely, was both a relief and a disappointment at the same time.

Severin patted his arm. "You do that. You ask Owun about a garden. Or maybe that young man Tarquin. He seems to have a lot of knowledge about things."

At the mention of Tarquin, Cloud felt unease clunk like a rock in his gut. Tarquin was the only other one who knew Cloud was living with Severin. He'd come up with Owun a couple times to help carry beams of wood for the hut. Cloud wished Owun hadn't asked him for help.

Cloud had learned that Tarquin was the son of a prestigious Roman centurion, but had been orphaned and grew up in Paris. For some unfathomable reason, Owun liked him. The fellow's arrogance rubbed Cloud the wrong way, his pretense of authority obnoxious. This was Gaul, not Rome, and Tarquin's high-ranking father was long dead. Yet he acted like Cloud's superior, even having the nerve to once call Cloud a *dispossessed want-to-be.*

Owun had assured Cloud that Tarquin was really friendly once you got to know him. Apparently he only came across as proud because, well, it was just the way he was, being the son of a centurion and *blah blah blah.* Cloud didn't care whether or not Tarquin was really friendly; he had no intention of getting to know him. All Cloud cared about concerning Tarquin was if the man could keep a secret. *This secret.* Eventually the gossip would find its way into Uncle Childebert's castle, if it hadn't already. If Cloud's uncles offered a reward in exchange for information, would Tarquin-the-Really-Friendly turn Cloud in for silver or gold?

There was no way to know.

Severin broke into his thoughts. "An old man is in need of some rest. Excuse me for a little while."

"Of course. Put in a word for me, will you?" Cloud knew that Severin's idea of *rest* was actually prayer. The hermit practically prayed all day.

"You know I always do." As Severin shuffled past Cloud's hut, Cloud surveyed the land for a suitable place for planting. Now that he had a roof of his own, he could focus on the next project. Hopefully Owun knew something about growing vegetables in ankle-deep mud. Because there was no way in the world Cloud intended to consult the know-it-all Roman about cabbage and legumes.

Cloud shook his head, trying to dismiss Tarquin's smirking face from his mind, and paced around his new yard. Hmm, the ground right here was a little harder. Maybe a few brave seeds could —

"Hello? Hello! Is this the right way? Are you up there?"

The call wafted from the gravel path.

Cloud froze.

The voice belonged to a female.

Chapter Twenty-One

Cloud watched as a small muddy dog materialized through the trees. The moment it spotted him, it bounded with glee across the yard. Its fur was jet black, its tail furiously wagging. Before Cloud could prevent it, the animal jumped on Cloud's legs, yipping and clawing, obviously begging to be picked up.

With a laugh, he scooped it up. The puppy licked his face. Its paws smeared mud across his chest.

"Zephyr, no! You'll get him all dirty!"

A young lady broke through the tree line, breathless, and rushed over. "Bad girl! Bad Zephyr!"

She reached Cloud and pried the squirming puppy from his arms. Then she swatted at Cloud's chest, ridding it of the mud. That accomplished, she blew out an exasperated huff. "I'm trying to teach her not to jump on people. She's going to be big someday and if she doesn't learn now —" She cut off her words, slapped a hand over her mouth, then said, "Oh, I'm so sorry, I forgot!" Still holding the wiggly puppy, she dipped to the ground in a curtsy. Then she flipped away one of the blonde braids that had fallen across her stunningly beautiful face and said, "You're probably wondering who I am. We've actually met before, believe it or not."

Cloud tried to hide the grin that was threatening to crack

open his jaw. "Wait, don't tell me!" He furrowed his brows, pretending to think. "You're not the same girl who owned a little white dog named Bree, are you?" His smile broke loose. "What is it with every introduction beginning with a canine attack?"

She pulled her eyebrows together in a giant question mark. "What's a canine?"

"A dog. In Latin."

"Huh." She frowned. "I don't know any Latin, but *canine* sounds cute." She stuck her face straight in the puppy's and cooed, "Hear that, Zeph? You're a canine. What do you think of that?" The puppy wildly licked her nose, making her break into giggles.

Suddenly her face fell and she looked up at Cloud. "You remember Bree, but you don't remember me?" A tiny sigh escaped her and something like disappointment filled her eyes.

Cloud had an unexpected impulse to give her a hug. He had to restrain himself. "I'm just teasing you, Genofeva! Of course I remember you!" He didn't add that he'd thought of her more times than he could count. "You saved my life. I could never forget you." Even if she hadn't saved his life, he doubted he'd be able to forget her. But of course he didn't say that either.

At his words, scarlet climbed up her cheeks. She cleared her throat and said in a suddenly shy voice, "I'm so happy you're alive, my lord prince. I prayed for your safety every single day. I . . . I always wondered what had happened to you." She gave him an embarrassed smile.

He nearly said, *I always wondered what happened to you too,* but that didn't seem appropriate. While he fished for something to say, an awkward silence descended. He had to say *something,* before it stretched too long. "So, what happened to Bree?" fell out of his mouth. "Is she still alive?"

Real smooth, Cloud. Inquire after her pet, not her.

She blinked, taken aback, and Cloud was sure he detected

hurt behind her eyes. Of all the dumb things he could have said.

"Um, no. She died a few years ago."

"Oh. I'm so sorry to hear that."

Another silence. He fumbled for something to say. This was going downhill fast.

"It's alright. Tarq's dog had puppies a few months ago and he gave me one."

Tarq? She wasn't talking about *Tarquin*, was she? She . . . knew him? *He gave her a dog?* Why did that information send a bolt of annoyance through Cloud? *Especially the nickname.*

"Actually, Tarq gave me two puppies. Noctis is mine and I asked him if I could give Zephyr to you." Genofeva stroked the wiggling ball of fur in her arms as she glanced around the lonely terrain. "When Tarq told me where you were, I thought you might get lonely out here. I hope you don't mind me bringing you a pet."

"What?" Anger flared through Cloud. "You mean *he* was the one who told you where I am? Not Owun?" Cloud's temperature spiked ten degrees. So the rotten Roman was talking after all. How many people had he told?

Not noticing how upset he was, Genofeva merely huffed and said, "Are you joking? Owun never tells me a thing. Rumors are flying that the heir of Orleans survived and came to Paris to start a war with King Childebert and King Clothaire. When I heard that, I wondered if you were back. Owun refused to talk, so I asked Tarq if he knew anything."

"And he told you everything?"

"Well, kind of." She shrugged, her eyes innocent. "It's not like I'm going to tell anyone."

That wasn't the point. Tarquin had told *her.* He couldn't keep a secret. But Cloud didn't want to blow up in front of Genofeva, so he stuffed down his temper before it flamed even more. Determined to rid the conversation of the Roman rat, he inhaled deeply, forced a smile, and said, "Zephyr and Noctis. Those are Latin words too. See, you *do* know some Latin! You told me you didn't."

"They're Latin? Really?"

"Yes. Noctis means night. And Zephyr means breeze. *Zephyrus* originally came from the Greek word, *zéphyros*."

Genofeva swiped a strand of escaped braid from her eyes. "That makes sense. They were born on a windy night."

Cloud was confused. "How did you name them if you didn't know the meanings?"

"I didn't name them. Tarq did."

Not him again! And why did she have to keep shortening his name like that?

She tilted her head and continued, "I thought the names were awfully pretty. Don't you think so? I had no idea they meant night and wind." Again, she went nose-to-nose with the dog and it mopped her face.

"Breeze. Not wind! Zephyr means a gentle breeze!" Cloud tried to hide the hostile edge from his voice. "There's a big difference. If they were born on a windy night, Tarquin should have named her Venti. Or even Ventus. But not Zephyr. Obviously his Latin isn't that good." He'd nearly said, *His Latin stinks*. But that would be childish and surly, and he was already starting to feel seriously immature right now. *Come on, it's just a word. Get a hold of yourself!*

Genofeva frowned and looked at him funny. "I think Zephyr is a lovely name." Then, this time an edge in *her* voice, she added, "Tarq was born in Rome. I'm sure he knows perfect Latin, my lord." She was defending him! With a little toss of her head, she added, "Probably better than you," making him feel like he'd been kicked in the gut.

Cuddling the puppy hard against her, she said, "If you don't want Zephyr, just say so. I can take her back to Tarq."

A strange feeling, almost panic, clutched him. "No, no! I'd love to keep her." He reached over and pulled the pup out of her arms. "That was so kind of you to think of me. Thank you." He thought to himself, *Definitely changing the dog's name. Take that, Tarq.*

"Oh my. What do we have here? A puppy?"

Severin's voice made them both jump.

The priest wandered over, a mile-wide grin on his face. "I thought I heard voices. What a beautiful wee dog." He stroked the black fur and glanced at Genofeva. "What's its name?"

Genofeva beamed. "Zephyr. It's a girl."

"Zephyr," Severin repeated, his eyes twinkling. "Hello, little Zephyr. Aren't you a sweetheart?"

So much for changing the mutt's name.

"I brought her as a gift for my lord prince. I didn't want him to be lonely up here."

Hearing her say that made something inside Cloud melt. Forget the Roman snitch. Genofeva had brought him *a gift*. His heart should be soaring.

But it wasn't. All Cloud felt was a sudden swirling mixture of confusion and guilt and . . . and jealousy. Dark, pouting, ugly jealousy. He'd never felt anything so strongly before. Shame gripped him.

He'd already given his life to God. He wanted to be a priest.

So why on earth was he feeling this way?

Chapter Twenty-Two

Cloud had been staring at the open book on the table for the last hour, struggling to concentrate. The volume was precious beyond words, one of the rarest possessions anyone could own. It had been a gift from Bishop Remigius, and Cloud treasured it more than anything. Usually he devoured the sacred words of the Gospels, but tonight he just couldn't focus. Genofeva had told him that rumors about him were exploding through the countryside. Owun warned the same thing. Surely his uncles had heard something by now. Dread and uncertainty sat in his stomach like a slab of heavy rock. Should he flee? Find another place to hide? Or bravely stay put, trusting in God? If only he knew what to do!

To make things worse, he couldn't stop daydreaming about Genofeva. It had been two weeks since she'd wandered up with Zephyr, and her brief visit had shattered all the peace he thought he'd found. She hadn't returned since. Part of him was immensely relieved, and another part fiercely disappointed. One thing was sure — it was harder to pray now. Every time Cloud tried, he felt nothing but emptiness. His visits to Saint Clement's Chapel brought him boredom and agonizing feelings of guilt. And Tarquin . . . *Don't even get started on Tarquin.* He'd spilled Cloud's whereabouts, potentially endangering his life. Then he'd had the gall to give Genofeva a puppy. And she called him by that ridiculous nickname. Cloud could still hear her saying, *'Tarq was born in Rome. I'm sure he knows perfect Latin, my lord. Probably better than you.'* Her tone had been defensive. Was she in love with the blabbermouth?

Cloud huffed. So what? Who cared? It had nothing to do with him.

Frustrated with himself, he pushed the flickering candle closer to the book and gently rifled through it. The Gospel of Saint Matthew fell open. He rubbed the back of his neck, drew a determined breath, and shoved Genofeva and Tarquin-the-Really-Friendly out of his mind. He started reading.

'Jesus saith to him: If thou wilt be perfect, go sell what thou hast, and give to the poor, and thou shalt have treasure in heaven: and come follow me.'

A memory flashed. That had been the story Sister Mena was telling her students, that morning so long ago in Rheims. Cloud remembered being the only one in the room who'd known how the story ended. The rich man refused, and walked away sad. Little did Cloud know, when he ran from that room, that Jesus would ask him the same thing. Well, *he* wouldn't refuse. He was on fire to follow Christ.

Genofeva's laughing face and blonde braids popped into his mind.

Alright, maybe not *on fire* so much anymore, but —

Cloud blew out an irritated breath and flipped to another random page of Matthew.

'Then Jesus saith to him: Put up again thy sword into its place: for all that take the sword shall perish with the sword.'

Zephyr let out a bark, then a menacing growl.

Startled, Cloud's gaze flew to the open door where the puppy had been napping a minute ago. She stood alert now, staring into the marsh. Her black tail had shot between her legs, and her ears were perked, listening intently. She barked, then growled again.

Someone was out there.

Trying to still the sudden slamming of his heart, Cloud closed his book of Gospels with a soft thump and snuffed out the candle. The hut plunged into shadowy darkness, the only light a wedge of yellow moonbeam peeking through the door. He quietly eased from the table and reached for his black cloak. He swiftly pulled its hood over his head and slipped beside Zephyr.

"What is it, Zeph? What's wrong?"

The puppy glanced at him, then whimpered. She scooted back from the opening.

It took a moment for Cloud's eyes to adjust to the darkness. When they did, he scanned the yard. The slope of the land made it impossible to see beyond the row of trees. Warm wind swayed their branches, but nothing else out of place moved.

"It's alright, Zeph. Nothing's out there." He bent to ruffle her fur and was about to close the door when a slurping noise down the hill arrested his attention. He froze. A boot stuck in mud? The slurping sounds were followed by rustling and the snapping of twigs. A splash, then a grunt. Muffled laughter. Someone hissed, "Shh!"

Cloud tried to stay calm. Was it Tarquin perhaps, playing a mean joke?

Or was this finally it? Had his uncles found Cloud's hideaway and sent their assassins to finish the botched job of nine years ago?

Cloud heard the crunch of gravel. They'd reached the path. Any minute now they'd spot the two huts and —

Severin! Cloud's thoughts raced to his mentor, and his heart stuttered in his chest. Severin was asleep in the tiny dwelling behind Cloud's. Would his uncles' henchmen kill him too?

A glow appeared between the trees. Torchlight danced. Two shadowy figures emerged. Cloud's heart stopped.

Both men had long hair! God have mercy! It was Uncle Clothaire and Uncle Childebert themselves!

Panic rising, Cloud spotted their swords. The weapons remained sheathed for the moment, but Cloud had no doubt they wouldn't stay sheathed long. The question was, what would they do to Severin after they killed Cloud?

His gaze lurched to Grandpere Clovis's massive sword hanging on the wall. The instinct to yank it down and fight his uncles was suddenly overwhelming. He was younger and he was fast, probably stronger than both of them combined, and Grimald had done nothing if not train him for war. He could slip out, sneak around, and surprise them from behind. With his black hooded cloak, they wouldn't even see him. How ironic would that be, butchering the two sons of Clovis with their own father's sword! Exactly what they'd done to Theodoald.

He stared at his weapon, heart thumping out of control. These were the monsters who had murdered his brothers. Uncle Clothaire was the villain who'd kidnapped Cloud's mother. These were the men who broke Grandmere Clothilde's heart. It would be so easy, so simple —

'Put up thy sword into its place: for all that take the sword shall perish with the sword.'

The sentence popped into his head. He'd just read that line a minute ago. The words of God Himself.

Yes, but wasn't it justice to —

'Come follow me, and thou shalt have treasure in heaven.'

Cloud had to clench both fists around the material of his cloak in order to quell the overpowering urge to snatch Grandpere's sword. His warrior blood had never coursed so fiercely through his veins as it did now.

But . . . what would Severin think? What would the saint do if he rushed outside to shouts and screams, only to find two men writhing in blood in the yard? And not just any writhing men, but

Gaul's reigning kings! The priest would be aghast. The country would be flung into unimaginable chaos. Wars would break out everywhere as greedy nobles scrambled for empty thrones. The dagger already in Grandmere Clothilde's heart would be twisted and wrenched and shoved in so hard she'd probably die.

Could Cloud bring himself to unleash all that horror and anguish across the kingdom?

'*Put up thy sword into its place.*'

Well, he hadn't taken it down yet, so he was already ahead of Christ's unmistakable orders. He forced himself to unclench his fists and release his breath. He lifted his right hand made the Sign of the Cross, begging for strength to do the right thing, to not let *The Gang* down.

Sudden peace spread over him, as familiar to him as his penitential hood. He would not disappoint Severin, would not topple the kingdom, would not further shatter Grandmere's already bruised heart. The sword on the wall had spilled far too much blood already. Cloud refused to stain it more.

Whispering a *Pater Noster* for courage to die bravely, Cloud did something he had not done in a decade. He reached up and jerked off his hood, finally allowing his long blond hair to tumble loose.

Shaking it out, he let it fall in royal splendor over his shoulders, matching that of the two kings closing in. He would meet the killers on the killers' terms. The kings sought a prince. A prince they would find.

Dragging a breath, Cloud gathered his courage and stepped out the door, unarmed, to meet certain death.

Chapter Twenty-Three

"So. The rumors are true. The heir of Orleans has finally come to claim his throne, huh?"

The voice was still too distant to recognize, but Cloud detected the sarcasm. Strangely, neither had yet drawn their swords. Maybe they were waiting till they actually reached him. Even from across the yard, they could surely see he was unarmed. Flames from the torch leapt and curled around them, illuminating long straggly hair and massive shoulders. For middle-aged men, both still looked surprisingly strong.

Instinctively, Cloud reached behind him and closed his door, leaving Zephyr safely inside. She couldn't protect him anyhow, and he didn't want the puppy hurt. Genofeva would be devastated if they tortured or killed the dog.

"You're sure it's him?"

"Duh. Look at the hair. Who else would it be? The Queen of Briton?" A pause, then a shout, "It's you, Cloud, right?"

Cloud frowned. He hadn't spoken to either uncle in nearly ten years, but the voice and manner sounded much younger than it should have.

"Yes, it's me." Cloud took a few uneasy steps forward, trying to discern their faces as they tromped towards him.

The one who'd called out slid slightly in the mud, slowing

him for a moment as he regained his footing. The other strutted forward, reaching Cloud first. His hand rested threateningly on his sword hilt. A sneer twisted his mouth. Icy eyes drilled into Cloud.

Cloud blinked. *Who on earth?*

He'd never seen this man in his life.

Actually, *man* wasn't even the word. With the fellow straight in his face, Cloud realized it was a youth. Huge for his age and arms like granite, but the sullen face looked too young to even grow a beard. Thirteen, maybe fourteen at most, this was a mere adolescent.

But — along with an attitude — he had waist-length hair, and a sword that could easily match Grandpere's. Young he may be, but he wasn't a nobody.

The other cleared the last few yards, and before Cloud had the chance to even glimpse his face, he whipped an arm around Cloud's throat and yanked him into a strangle-hold. Cloud gasped for air, fighting to breathe. Then the man rubbed his hair hard with a fist, and suddenly released him. "Well, look who's all grown up!"

Cloud stumbled, dazed from the attack. It took a second for recognition to dawn. *"Charibert?"*

"No. The Queen of Briton."

Cloud couldn't help himself. He clasped his cousin in a hug. "I can't believe it's you."

"And *I* can't believe you've managed to stay alive."

The young one snorted with disdain. "What is this, a lovers' reunion?"

"Oh, go gag yourself, Chram."

Ignoring the dagger-like look he got, Charibert cast a glance around. "I don't think we were followed, but it's dangerous for us to be here. Can we talk inside? Is anyone in there?"

"Just my dog."

An amused grunt came from the one named Chram. "A prince with a poochy. How sweet."

This time Charibert's face darkened and he swung around like he might hit him. "I said, shut up. Your mouth is going to get you killed some day." He shook his head, sighed, and added, "I mean it, Chram. Cloud could eat you for breakfast. And if he does, don't expect me to save you."

There was a strained silence as the two stared each other down. Then Charibert blew out an exasperated breath, rolled his eyes, and looked back at Cloud. "Are we going inside, or not?"

Cloud hesitated. He didn't mind letting his cousin in, but he wasn't sure he wanted the sulky adolescent. Who even was he? Obviously a prince, but from where? Whose son?

Charibert must have seen Cloud's reluctance, because he said, "The most glaringly royal thing about my brother is that he's a huge royal pain. Just ignore him."

Cloud felt his eyes widen. "He's your brother?"

"Rotten luck, I know."

Chram scowled. "*Half* brother."

Tingles crawled up Cloud's spine. "Whose side?"

"The king's," Chram said with a cold smile. His answer confirmed Cloud's growing unease. That made Chram Uncle Clothaire's son.

This was not good.

Cloud knew that Charibert had several half-siblings. Uncle Clothaire had lots of women. Cloud's mother, to his sorrow, had been one of them after Father died. A shocking thought jumped out at him and his heart skipped a beat. Surely Chram couldn't be —

"No, Cloud." Charibert let out a laugh. "I can read your mind. He isn't your brother too."

Chram spit on the ground, as if the mere thought of sharing a mother with Cloud was so far beneath him to be disgusting. His arms remained crossed, his baby face still smirking.

Charibert added, "But I'll give him to you if you want him."

Cloud couldn't resist a grin. "I'll pass."

Charibert sighed. "That's what everyone says." Then, ignoring the obvious hatred that flared across Chram's face, Charibert's expression turned serious. "Let's get inside where it's safe. Our father is searching for you. Thankfully he doesn't know where you are."

Chram added quietly, "Yet."

Was that a threat?

Chapter Twenty-Four

Cloud stared at Charibert seated across the table from him and struggled to wrap his head around the shocking proposition. Was he understanding this correctly?

"You're asking me to help you and your brother *murder* your father?"

Charibert ran a hand through his hair and sighed in exasperation. "Murder's a strong word, Cloud. We're not asking you to murder anyone. We're asking you to join us in war."

"Against your own father?"

"Well . . . yes."

"Which means you want him killed?"

Charibert shrugged. "You're making too much of it. If he dies in battle, he dies in battle. It happens all the time. Killing on a battlefield is a different thing from *murder*."

Cloud rubbed the back of his neck. "But, your cause is completely unjust! You can't just go and wipe out your father because you suddenly decide you want his throne." He was dismayed that Charibert would even hatch such a wicked plot, much less expect Cloud to join him.

"I didn't just *suddenly* decide anything. This has been brewing for years, Cloud. The pieces are finally falling into place and Chram and I are gathering an army. We want you to join us.

The benefits would be mutual — you help us defeat our father, and we'll give you your kingdom back."

A few feet away, Chram glanced up from Grandpere's sword in his hands, which he'd brazenly taken down from the wall without asking. He'd been standing there silently examining it, handling it as if it were his own. Despite his silence, his oppressive moodiness filled the hut like a bad stench. "I thought you wanted our father dead," he said. His voice held a dare. "That's why you returned to Paris, to kill him and Uncle Childebert. Everyone knows that."

"No one knows anything. Except the gossip. I came to Paris for my own reasons. They don't include revenge."

Charibert huffed out a breath and shifted in his seat. "Come on, Cloud. You can't tell me you returned here in peace. What, have you forgotten your brothers' murders? Do you really expect us to believe you didn't come here for our father's and Uncle Childebert's blood?" Before Cloud could answer, Charibert raised his hands with innocence. "Hey, I don't blame you one bit. Your kingdom was stolen, your life destroyed. I can't even believe you've survived so long without being found. You have every right to kill the men who did this to you. They deserve to die. They're demons."

Charibert was talking about his own father. Unbelievable. Even if it was true.

"I'm practically giving you your kingdom back, Cloud. Think about it. How many kings would do that?"

"You're not a king."

"I will be. As soon as my father's out of the way."

Cloud glanced at Chram across the shadowy room. Chram was siding with his brother for now, but Cloud wondered if the boy intended to murder Charibert as soon as their father was dead, and steal the crown himself. He wasn't in the direct line, having a different mother, but that had never stopped anyone before.

Charibert went on. "I risked my life to save you, Cloud. I could have easily turned you in all those years ago. But I helped you escape, even though it would have meant death for me if anyone found out I helped you. Now I'm asking you a favor."

His words were like a knife in the gut. It was true, Cloud owed his life to Charibert. But he didn't like the sound of this. It was unjust war. He felt trapped. "Where does Uncle Childebert fit in?" he asked, hoping to somehow find a way out.

Charibert and Chram both snorted and answered, practically together, "He wants our father dead too."

Uncle against uncle, brother against brother, father against sons. Cloud felt a pang of sadness. None of this was pleasing to God. But it had always been this way among kings and princes. Cloud wanted nothing to do with it. His yearning to quit the world grew stronger with each sentence his cousins uttered.

"Are you joining forces with Uncle Childebert then?" he asked.

Impatience filled Charibert's eyes and he leaned closer to Cloud over the table. "Don't be so stupid. Why would we side with him? After Father is dead, Uncle Childebert is the next target."

Good God! Charibert planned to wipe him out too and take all of Gaul for himself. Cloud had to get out of this evil plan. "Why do you need my help if you're already gathering an army?"

Across the hut, Chram must have had enough, because he exploded. He stormed to the table, eyes blazing. "Because we need the people of Orleans behind us, that's why! If you think it's because we like you, you're insane!" He gripped Grandpere's sword — *Cloud's* sword — with such violence his hands shook. "We hate you. We hate your family line. I'd kill you right here if my brother would let me."

"Chram, stop! This isn't the way to get Cloud to —"

But the boy's rage spewed out. "I'd slit your throat in a heartbeat, son of Clodomir. The only reason I'm not is because we need you to get Orleans on our side, and you're the heir."

Cloud should have felt anger at Chram's outburst. But, to his surprise, all he felt was compassion. What had happened to make his young cousin so bitter, so violent, so thoroughly filled with hatred? Cloud had a vague remembrance of Chram as a baby. He would've been perhaps four years old when Cloud escaped to Rheims. It wasn't hard to imagine the kind of life Chram had lived, growing up in Uncle Clothaire's castle. Impurity and vice and bloodshed would have surrounded the child, suffocating him at every turn. Chram obviously despised his father enough to help start an uprising against him. He was willing to ride to war at a tragically young age, ready to slay the man who'd given him life. Cloud's heart went out to him. God alone knew what abuses the boy had survived.

"Do you ever visit Grandmere?" The soft words just came out.

A baffled frown crossed Chram's face at the change of subject. "*What?* What are you talking about?"

"Our grandmother. Queen Clothilde. I think she could help you."

Chram glared. "Help me with what?" he snarled. "Overthrowing my father? You're demented."

Charibert said quietly, "Chram's never met her."

"Oh." Cloud felt a pang of loss for his young cousin. He himself had been so blessed, so unspeakably favored by God, to have been raised by a saint. *Two* saints, actually, when he counted Bishop Remigius. He shuddered to think what he would be like, had his father King Clodomir not died, had he and Theodoald and Gunther not been given over to the care of Grandmere Clothilde when they were so young. He wondered if he'd be as brutal and corrupt and bloodthirsty today as his cousin Chram. Probably. He thanked God with all his heart that he'd been spared.

He turned to Charibert. "Take him to Lutece, Charibert. Let him meet Grandmere. I mean that."

Charibert squirmed in his seat and averted his eyes. The mention of Grandmere obviously pricked something in his conscience. That wasn't a good sign. It proved that deep down Charibert knew the evilness of what he was scheming, yet intended to go ahead with it anyhow. Cloud would bet his kingdom that Grandmere Clothilde knew nothing of her two grandsons' plans for war.

After an uncomfortable silence, Charibert changed the subject back. "What Chram says is true. We need you. The people of Orleans know you're alive and hiding. They've been waiting for years for you to reappear and take back your father's castle and lands. They'll rally behind you as their rightful king. But us? They see us as usurpers. They'll never fight for us."

Chram stepped closer and leaned on the table, getting straight in Cloud's face.

"If you refuse to help us, don't be surprised if our father mysteriously learns where you are." His mouth twisted into a smile. "Just think about *that*, son of Clodomir."

Chapter Twenty-Five

"Severin, I don't know what to do." Cloud stabbed his shovel into the dirt and slumped against its handle. "Last night seems so unreal. How can my cousins be plotting this? What am I meant to do?"

The priest looked up from where he was pressing hopeful seedlings into the ground nearby. "God will let you know the right thing, my child. He allowed them to find you here. That wasn't by mere chance, you know."

Cloud thought, *'Obviously it wasn't chance; it was Tarquin's big mouth,'* but there was no point getting upset about that now. Even if the Roman hadn't blabbed to half the town, Charibert would have found Cloud eventually. It was only a matter of time. He was only too grateful it had been his cousins who showed up, not his uncles.

"But God is silent, Severin. I have no idea what He expects me to do." Discouragement and uncertainty filled him. After Charibert and Chram left, Cloud had walked to Saint Clement's Chapel and spent the rest of the night in prayer. But no thoughts of guidance had come, no hint of what God Almighty wanted.

He searched the holy hermit's face. "The kingdom of Orleans belonged to my father. It's supposed to pass to me. It was only through treachery that my uncles stole it. Charibert told me that the people there are begging for my return."

Severin nodded. "That is true. I have heard the same thing. The citizens are clamoring for their rightful king."

Confusion wrenched Cloud's insides. He thought of Bishop Remigius, who was truly a saint, yet had spent the last nine years preparing Cloud, not for a quiet life of prayer, but for warfare, to conquer Orleans. Grandmere Clothilde, too, apparently wanted nothing more than to see Cloud take his father's throne.

He sighed. "But I don't want Orleans, Severin. I want to stay here with you, and God." He thought of the white habit he'd been secretly sewing for himself in his hut the last few days. The idea had come to him in prayer last week. He'd given Owun his last money from Bishop Remigius to buy the material. Cloud hadn't told Severin about it yet, but planned to ask the priest to bless it when it was done. He'd chosen white for purity. He was so tired of black, always wearing this depressing hooded cloak.

He fisted his fingers into its material, wishing he knew what God wanted. Was it His holy will for Cloud to keep hiding and live a life of prayer and penance? Or to join Charibert and claim the kingdom that everyone wanted him to rule?

"What would you do," he asked the priest, "if you were me?"

The priest let out a gentle chuckle. "Oh Cloud. I cannot answer these things for you. I am not a prince. My birth, my vocation, my circumstances, are as far removed from yours as the sky is from the sea. You certainly have a right to claim your throne. To do so is not in any way an offense to God. It's simply a different way of giving yourself to His service." He paused, then added, "And the people of Orleans — especially the poor and oppressed — are right in their desire to have their true king reign over them."

Cloud's heart twisted. "But . . . but what about the rich young man in the Gospel?"

Severin shrugged, but his eyes held deep sympathy. "He was

rich, yes. But nowhere does Scripture say he was a prince."

This conversation wasn't going the way Cloud wanted. "You're telling me I should fight?"

Severin raised his hands in surrender. "I'm telling you nothing, my son. You alone must decide."

"But Charibert's war is wrong."

"Indeed. He's intending to take a kingdom that isn't yet his."

Well, none of this was helpful. Cloud exhaled in exasperation, and returned his attention to the shovel. He scooped up another pile of soil, which they had collected over the last days, and tossed it towards the emerging garden plot.

"Cloud?"

He looked over at his friend. Severin's smile was tinged with compassion. "Your grandmother, Clothilde, never wanted to be a queen." He slapped the dirt off his hands and stood up, obviously preparing to tell a story.

Once again, Cloud stuck the shovel in the dirt, and waited.

"As a young princess, your grandmother desired more than anything to enter a convent. Even when she was a small child, her piety earned her the nickname *the little nun.* Everyone was sure she was destined for the cloister. Her sister, Princess Sedeleube, was opposite her in every way. *She* seemed the one who would definitely get married, not your grandmother."

Cloud had not heard this story about Grandmere before. He leaned on the shovel, listening.

"But God's ways are not our ways. Princess Sedeleube not only ended up in a convent, but became the prioress. Your grandmother longed to join her. Then God intervened. Your grandfather, King Clovis, heard of Clothilde's beauty and sent messengers to Burgundy to ask for her in marriage. Now remember, your grandfather was not a Christian back then. He was rough and violent, a warrior through and through. Your grandmother recoiled at the idea of marriage to *anyone,* let alone a pagan king! Heartbroken by his proposal, she spent all night in the church, crying and distressed. She begged God to not lay the cross of marriage upon her shoulders."

Cloud had never met Grandpere Clovis, who died years before Cloud's birth, but he knew Grandmere had loved her husband dearly. She rode with him to his battle camps, braving danger and enduring exhaustion to stay at his side. She converted him to Christianity by her tireless example and prayers. She nursed him at his death. Grandmere was devoted to Grandpere and to his kingdom with every ounce of her being. Cloud struggled to imagine her young and in anguish, weeping in a cold, dark church, pleading with God to save her from marriage.

"So why did she agree to marry him?"

"Because in that night of desperate prayer, God showed her His holy will, and she was brave enough, and loved Him enough, to accept it. Your grandmother realized that God was not calling her to live peacefully in a cloister. She would serve Him better by sacrificing her own will and embracing the state of life that made her soul shudder. Sometimes a palace, with all its noise and worldliness and violent affairs, is exactly the cloister where God wants to enclose certain souls."

Cloud tried to imagine living the rest of his life in Father's castle. Sumptuous meals, servants, soft garments. Gold. Lots of it. Chests overflowing. *He could help the poor.*

And power. Unlimited. He would control the fate of thousands. *The good he could do!*

He pictured taking a wife. Having children.

Genofeva plopped straight into his mind. For a second his heart beat faster. Would she —

No, forget it. He shoved the fantasy away. Kings couldn't marry peasants. End of story.

"I'm not saying, Cloud, that this is what God necessarily wants from you. But seek *His* will, not your own. He will show you the path you are meant to take."

Cloud raised his eyes and they shot unbidden towards Saint Clement's Chapel again. Christ was there, hidden in the tabernacle, waiting to help. He had not enlightened Cloud last night, but would He do so today?

Please God, he pleaded, *show me what to do.*

* * * * *

Darkness had fallen by the time Cloud plodded back to his hut. His mouth was dry from thirst; his eyes felt gritty from lack of sleep the night before.

When he opened the door, he found, to his surprise, Severin sitting at his table. A prayer book lay open in his hands. Zephyr curled in his lap, asleep. A bowl of food was waiting.

The priest's head popped up when Cloud entered. Zephyr jerked awake, tail wagging.

Cloud squared his shoulders with resolve. "Severin, I think I know God's will. But I'm going to need your help."

The priest simply nodded.

"When you go to the water well in the morning, would you be able to get a secret message to my cousin Charibert? I need him to collect some things for you to bring to me."

"I could try. I have trustworthy connections who will certainly know how to get a message to the prince."

"Good. That's what I need. People who won't talk." Cloud's insides twisted. Was this truly the right thing to do? "Tell Charibert to bring you the royal robes that belonged to my father. And an ermine mantle and golden band for my hair. Our grandmother will know where to find everything."

Severin nodded again.

Cloud hesitated. "And my father's crown. I want that brought to the water well too."

Resignation filled the old man's eyes. But Cloud thought he detected a tinge of sadness too. "As you wish, my son."

"And I have one more favor to ask. Do you happen to know the bishop of Paris? I mean, personally? I'm going to need his help."

This time Severin smiled. "I know him indeed. He's a dear friend of mine."

"Can you talk to him for me?"

The priest looked baffled, but he said, "Of course."

Cloud suddenly felt shaky. He was overtired. He needed a meal. He needed sleep. But there was too much to do. His plan would have to be executed in the next couple days, if it were to work at all.

Chapter Twenty-Six

The hardest part had been saying good-bye to Severin.

Cloud hadn't realized the depth of their friendship until he saw the dampness in the old priest's eyes and felt the same in his own. It was possible they would never see each other again, and that brought pain. But it was for the priest's protection. No matter what happened, Cloud wanted him safe.

As Cloud had stepped out the door with his meager belongings stuffed in a sack, Severin had assured him with a smile and a fatherly embrace that his plan was not only heroic, but would bring God great glory and joy. That was all the assurance Cloud needed. His heart could finally beat in peace.

Yet now, hours later, as he stood on the steps of the overflowing church, bulging with priests and monks and Gaul's highest officials, his courage wavered. From the carriages and horses lining the road and the swarm of bodies that he could see beyond the massive open doors, it looked like every cleric in the country had gathered for this ceremony. It was unlikely that Uncle Childebert or Uncle Clothaire had come, neither of them caring for the things of God, but certainly princes and noblemen were among those crowded inside. Word of what Cloud was about to do would explode through the country with the speed of a swift arrow.

Apart from the jewel-studded crown — which would doubtless be recognized as that of King Clodomir, Cloud's father — and the white folded material upon which it rested in Cloud's trembling hands, all of his possessions were wrapped in his black cloak and hidden behind a nearby building. He'd tied up Zephyr beside the bundle, not so much to guard his things, but because he didn't know what else to do with her. She couldn't enter the church with him. He was already going to create the stir of the century; bringing a rambunctious puppy inside would only add another unwelcome layer of drama.

Cloud inhaled, trying to muster the courage to go through with this. Transferring the crown and bulky cloth to one arm, he nervously adjusted the golden clasp on his royal ermine mantle and smoothed his long flowing hair. Grandpere's sword, sharpened and polished to perfection, hung majestically at his side. Incredibly, no one had noticed him standing here on the steps, dressed as a king. The street was empty of passers-by; the whole city seemed crammed inside, focused on the Mass with its heart-soaring chant. It wasn't every day the bishop of Paris graced this humble church with his presence. No wonder nobody bothered to glance outside.

Cloud was grateful that Severin was friends with the bishop. Had that not been the case, this daring plan could never work. But Severin had happily helped arrange everything.

Cloud listened, heart pounding violently, as the last swelling notes of the Credo died down, the organ quieted, and several hundred people scuffed into their seats. This was it. Time to move. The Offertory was about to begin, the solemn part of the Mass where the Holy Sacrifice was prepared. Soon Christ Himself, the eternal King of kings, would be immolated upon the altar. Those hundreds of noblemen, peasants, and priests shuffling into their seats didn't realize it, but the long-lost prince of Orleans was about to offer his own immolation too.

Cloud knew the bishop was now waiting for his entrance. This moment had been prearranged. It was now or never. No turning back.

Checking one last time that his royal robe draped perfectly in place, Cloud whispered a prayer for Heaven's help and climbed the last few steps. He entered the church.

For the first moment or two, he had to press his way through the sea of bodies, but within seconds the sight of his majestic mantle, colossal sword, and golden crown in his hands sent a wave of gasps and whispers ahead of him, immediately parting the crowd. His pulse racing, Cloud strode the length of the suddenly-empty aisle, amid turned heads and shocked murmurs.

He forced himself to keep his eyes straight ahead, on the altar and the bishop. The temptation to glance around was fierce. Who was present watching this? Uncle Clothaire or Uncle Childebert? Most likely not. But some of their soldiers might be. Would they recognize Cloud as Clodomir's surviving son? *Definitely.* Would violence break out, blood be shed? *Maybe.* And what about Charibert? Was he here? What would his reaction be? Shock? Understanding? Rage?

Was Genofeva in the church?

Irritation at the sudden thought of her rippled through Cloud. What was wrong with him? No matter what happened today, or what happened tomorrow, or what happened for the rest of his life, Genofeva could never be part of it. Annoyed at himself for thinking of her, he shoved her beautiful face out of his mind and locked his eyes on the bishop.

The prelate, in on the plan, was prepared. While Cloud made his way across the now deathly quiet church, the bishop instructed the baffled servers to move his elaborately carved chair and a small table to the spot where Cloud would enter the sanctuary. They scrambled to obey. After the furniture was in place, the bishop sat down and waited.

Expectant silence hung heavy as the confused sea of people watched Cloud reach the prelate.

The two princes faced each other — a prince of the Church and the heir of Orleans. Dropping to his knees before the higher prince, Cloud held out Father's dazzling crown. Trying not to smile, Severin's old friend nodded in acceptance of Cloud's offering. His wrinkled hands lifted the crown from the folded white material and carefully placed it on the little table beside his chair. The servers watched with wide-eyed confusion.

Setting the folded swath of cloth on the floor next to where he knelt, Cloud unbuckled Grandpere's sword. He could imagine the craned necks, the bewildered frowns, the curious exchanging of glances of the hundreds of people packed in the church. Whispers broke out. Chair legs scuffed as people jockeyed for a better view. *What on earth was going on*, they must be wondering. Ignoring the increasing noise behind him, Cloud laid the sword at the bishop's feet.

The prince of the Church nodded his encouragement and a smile spread across his face.

Heart galloping, Cloud quickly unfastened his royal cloak, slid it from his shoulders, and surrendered that too. There was no going back now. He swiped up the folded material beside him and shook it out, unfurling the white habit that he'd sewn.

The muffled voices behind him grew louder, more disturbed. People started talking out loud. Footsteps and gasps and even a few shouts of objection echoed through the nave.

Before anyone could intervene, Cloud whipped out the scissors he'd tucked in his belt, yanked off his tunic, and jerked the habit on. Then he held the scissors out and bowed his head.

A collective gasp went up as the bishop of Paris took the scissors.

He did the unthinkable.

He cut off Cloud's hair.

By nightfall, all of Gaul would know that the Prince of Orleans existed no more.

135

Chapter Twenty-Seven

It felt strange to finally feel a breeze across his head, as he walked shorn and hoodless through the street in his new white habit. It felt even stranger to be back in Rheims. But this wouldn't take long. Cloud had one quick task to do here, then he could leave, and never be seen by the world again.

Thank goodness.

As the ecclesiastical palace came into view, Cloud expected a rush of memories, a swirl of emotions, or, if nothing else, at least sadness that saintly Bishop Remigius was no longer there. But, to his surprise, he felt nothing. It was as if everything of his past life, including his nine years of virtual imprisonment here in Rheims, had been cut away when the scissors took his hair a few days ago. A brand new life spread before him. Never again would he hide, nor fear his uncles. He had relinquished to them everything they wanted. They no longer had reason to need him dead. Orleans was theirs; they could have it. Or Charibert could have it. Let other men wrangle for thrones and power. Let them wallow in the glitter and gold and empty pleasures in their palaces. Cloud wanted only to think of God, to live each hour, each moment, for Him alone, and to pray for the salvation of those far from His grace, especially his own relatives. The kingdom of Orleans and the affairs of the world were no longer

Cloud's domain. Jesus had invited him, a rich young man, and Cloud had responded. His soul should be soaring.

But it wasn't. He felt numb. He suspected he knew why.

Genofeva.

She had been there.

Cloud had caught a glimpse of her in the crush of people exiting the church after Mass. He hadn't seen her face; she was too far away. She'd been clinging to Tarquin's arm as the crowd surged through the doors. Cloud wasn't sure what bothered him more — that he hadn't seen her expression and couldn't gauge her reaction to what he'd just done, or that she'd been holding onto Tarquin.

It bothered him that it bothered him. For the hundredth time in the last few days, Cloud pushed Genofeva from his mind. He would never know what emotions she'd felt as she watched him publicly renounce his royal birthright, changing from a prince to a nobody in the space of a few tense heartbeats. Why did he care what she thought? Genofeva was a mere acquaintance, someone he'd met on two occasions. If anything, Cloud should be more concerned about Charibert's reaction. Even if his cousin hadn't been in the church, certainly by now Charibert had heard everything. Would there be a backlash?

And what about Grandmere Clothilde?

Cloud paused on the road to calm himself. Word would have sped to Grandmere's castle within hours. Would she be disappointed in Cloud? With his dramatic action, he had shattered beyond repair Grandmere's dreams of his ever taking Father's throne. Dare he hope that, rather than being disappointed, she would be proud of him? Severin had recounted the story to him of how Grandmere had longed to renounce her own royalty and give her life to God. In the end, she hadn't. At least not in the way she'd wanted to. But maybe, *just maybe,* given the same circumstances as Cloud, the princess of

Burgundy would have done exactly what he had done.

The thought came to him that if Grandmere had followed her own desires and entered a convent, Cloud would not exist. His father and brothers, likewise, would never have been born. King Clovis would have taken a different wife and Gaul would probably not be a Christian country today. Grandmere's heroic sacrifice had brought an entire land to Christ.

Doubts niggled Cloud. Had he done the right thing in renouncing his kingdom? Had he truly done God's will . . . or merely his own? His only comfort came from knowing that Severin, a saint, had approved.

An excited bark from Zephyr snapped him from his thoughts. Three little girls in shabby clothes, skipping hand in hand, appeared in the street from a side alley. A small boy scampered to keep up with them. All four were bone-thin and grubby, but their smiles stretched ear to ear. Zephyr tugged on the rope around her neck, straining to break free from Cloud. Her black tail wagged wildly with excitement. It was obvious the puppy wanted to join the children. Of course she did. Puppies and children always went together.

Which was the very reason Cloud had returned to Rheims today. He'd come to find the children. And here they were, skipping straight towards him. Obviously they weren't the same children as a decade ago, but Rheims, like every city, would sadly never lack orphans.

Cloud waved to get their attention. Zephyr was the magnet. Immediately all four youngsters raced over.

"Can we pet your dog?"

"Of course you can."

With giggles and coos, they poured over the dog. Zephyr squirmed in ecstasy, her tail wagging a hundred miles a minute. Seeing the bliss in the children's eyes, Cloud knew he'd made the right decision in bringing Zephyr to Rheims. Genofeva might be sad, or even offended, by what he was about to do, but that didn't matter. It was better for everyone.

"There was a lady who lived here several years ago," Cloud said as the children took turns hugging Zephyr. "Her name was Sister Mena. I don't suppose any of you know if she's still around?"

All four exchanged glances, then bobbed their heads.

"She teaches people about God," the smallest girl said. "Both her and Sister Ana. We love them!"

Sister Mena was still here. *Thank You, God.* Another holy lady had obviously joined her. Cloud felt a pop of happiness. How good Jesus was to send teachers to the youngsters of Rheims. Cloud had no doubts that both Sisters were part of *The Gang.*

"I came to bring Sister Mena a gift. Can you give it to her for me?"

Again, they nodded in unison.

"What is it?"

"My puppy. Her name is Zephyr."

Their eyes bugged.

"You're giving her to Sister Mena and Sister Ana?"

"Yes." Cloud bent down to rub behind Zephyr's ears. "I'm sure she'd much rather be around children than live with boring old me."

At his announcement, one of the girls let out a squeal, spun around, and hugged her friend. They danced in a little circle with glee. The third girl swooped Zephyr into her arms and the boy stuck his face nose-to-nose with the pup, exactly like Genofeva had done. Zephyr's tongue mopped his face, making everyone laugh.

"Do you think Sister Mena and Sister Ana would like her? They can take care of her, right?"

"Oh yes! We'll help them! They'll love her!"

"Well then, she's all yours."

A tiny pang of sadness rose up inside Cloud. Funny how quickly he'd become attached to the little creature. But Zephyr belonged with children. Besides, keeping her would only remind him of Genofeva, and Cloud didn't need that.

"Are you sure?"

Cloud smiled. "I'm sure."

The biggest girl said, "Sister will ask who gave her to us. What do we say?"

Reluctant to reveal his identity, which would surely attract unwanted attention in Rheims, Cloud thought for a moment. What could he call himself that only Sister would understand? The first thought that leapt into his mind was *the rich young man*. It was the story she had been telling when he met her.

Yet surely Sister Mena had met other young men over the years who had given up wealth to follow Christ. She could easily know dozens. Besides, the man in the Gospel had walked *away* from God, not towards Him.

Hmm, what could Cloud say, without giving his real name?

It struck him that while he might not be the only rich young man she'd run across, he was most certainly the only one of royalty.

It came to him in flash.

"Tell Sister Mena I'm the prince who traded kingdoms. She'll know *exactly* who I am."

Four Years Later

Chapter Twenty-Eight

Severin had warned him that this would happen sooner or later. It had been during the last conversation they'd had.

"People will find you, Cloud. No matter how deep into the wilderness you go, there is no escape. Hermits are seen as strange creatures. Curiosity draws most of the people who ferret them out." Severin's eyes had twinkled with mischief. "And what could be more curious than a prince living in a shack and wearing a snowy-white habit?" He patted Cloud's arm. "When it happens — and it *will* happen — remember to welcome your visitors as Christ Himself. True, many will come at first merely to gawk at the novelty of a hermit-prince, but eventually others will come with holy motives. You'll see."

The way he'd said it made Cloud suspect it was a prophecy. After all, Severin had the power of miracles.

The saint had spoken those prophetic words four years ago, on the morning of Cloud's departure from their huts in the marsh. They'd been leaving the chapel of Saint Clement together, after Cloud took a vow in front of the Blessed Sacrament to never shed blood. It was the last time he was to see his holy friend.

Ironically, the very first person who had found Cloud, here in the forest outside Paris, had brought the sad news of Severin's death. That had been a few months ago. After that day, more and more visitors trickled in. Every time Cloud heard a knock on the door of his hovel, disrupting his beloved study of the scriptures, he forced himself to think, *Here comes Christ.* He usually couldn't stop the affectionate eye-roll and the added thought, *Severin must have sent Him. Again!* Cloud could picture his friend sitting around in Heaven sharing a conspiratorial wink with Jesus.

Well, he reminded himself as he headed across the room to open the door for the fourth time this week, his blessed solitude was a gift from God and not something to be hoarded selfishly. If Christ wanted to pop in every now and then to interrupt Cloud's prayers, so be it.

Only this time, when he opened the door, the condition of the visitor startled him. An elderly man stood there, his clothes so threadbare he might as well be naked. He shivered in the chilly morning air.

"Please, sir, a few coins for the love of God, to help me on my travels."

This beggar hadn't come to gawk at a prince. His request for alms was genuine.

"I'm sorry. I have no money." Cloud opened the door wide and invited, "But come inside, please my friend, and get warm."

* * * * *

The food was nothing fancy, just a few vegetables and herbs from Cloud's garden, but from the way his guest dug in, it could have been a king's banquet. Now, an hour later, the traveler was fed and full and smiling.

But the air outside remained cold.

"I can't send you away in those clothes," Cloud said. "You need something better in this chilly weather." He looked around. His old black cloak hung on a nail on the wall.

Cloud occasionally used it as a blanket, but hadn't worn it in years. He would be only too glad to get rid of the thing. He strode across the tiny room and lifted it down. "Here, take this. I don't need it anymore." He brought it over and draped it around the man's thin body.

A smile lit up the other's face. "Why, thank you, kind sir. I am indebted."

"You're most welcome."

"I have a grandson in Burgundy," the man said unexpectedly. Just as quickly, his smile faded. "I'm hoping he will agree to take me in."

Cloud frowned. Burgundy was a long way away. "Do you have a place to stay tonight? You can stay here."

The man dismissed the offer with a wave of his hand. "No, no. You've already helped me enough. I'm sure I'll find lodging in Paris."

Cloud wasn't so confident about that. With no money, lodging would be hard to come by. "I have a friend near there. I'm sure he'll let you stay with his family, if you tell him I sent you. His name is Owun."

Cloud had no idea why he was saying this. The words just popped out, as if someone else had put them in his head. He hadn't seen Owun in years. Was Owun even near Paris these days? He could be anywhere! Even if Owun remained living at his family's hut, Cloud had no clue where the place was. He'd been there only once, when he was nine years old, fleeing in terror from Uncle Childebert's castle. He could never find the place again, much less give someone directions! But, despite all this, the suggestion dropped out of his mouth of its own accord.

The smile returned to the old man's face. "Oh, God bless you, sir! Tell me where he lives, and I will head there now."

Then the strangest thing happened. Cloud gave directions. Clear, precise directions.

Equally amazing, the traveler nodded, taking the complicated route in as easily as if the destination was right next door.

How could Cloud be saying this? How could the man be remembering?

Yet by the time his guest stood outside the door, wrapped in Cloud's hooded cloak and ready to leave, Cloud was one hundred percent certain he would find Owun without difficulty.

Before he turned to leave, the man said, "You never told me your name, kind sir. Who shall I tell your friend sent me?"

"Cloud. Tell him it was Cloud."

Chapter Twenty-Nine

"My lord! My lord Cloud!"

Startled by both the shout and the title of royal address, Cloud looked up from weeding his patch of vegetables and turned his head towards the voice. A man, breathless and panting, jogged at him through the woods.

"I can't believe I found you, my lord!" Too out of breath to run further, the man stopped for a moment, resting his hands on his knees. His body seemed to heave from exhaustion. He must have been running the whole way. Even without seeing his face, recognition shot through Cloud.

"Owun? Oh my goodness, is that you?" Dropping the weed in his hand, Cloud rose from his knees, brushed the dirt from his white habit, and hurried across the yard.

Still panting, Owun straightened, then dropped to one knee. "My lord! Your cloak!" he blurted. "It's a miracle! Last night —"

"Don't kneel to me. I'm not your lord." Cloud tugged him to his feet.

"But your cloak!" Owun repeated, his eyes wide with wonder. "That man you sent to my parents' house —" The words were tumbling out breathlessly. "You worked a miracle, my lord! You have to come with me!"

"What? What in heavens are you talking about?" *A miracle?*

Cloud frowned. Of course he hadn't worked a miracle. That was the most absurd thing he'd ever heard in his life.

But Owun continued staring at him with awe. What was going on?

"The man you sent to our place yesterday. He was wearing your old black cloak!"

"Yes, I know. I gave it to him."

Owun's eyes would burst if they got any bigger. More jumbled words poured out. "During the night, our hut started glowing. It was so bright it woke my parents and me up. At first we were frightened; we had no idea what it was. Then Pap saw that the light poured from under Genofeva's door. Well, not actually hers anymore; she's gone now. But it was her room where the man was asleep."

Confusion tightened Cloud's chest.

"When Pap opened the door, your cloak was glowing. We felt . . . we felt . . . I can't even describe it! It was like Heaven was in the room! Like Christ Himself was —" Suddenly overcome with emotion, Owun fell back to his knees in front of Cloud.

Cloud yanked him back up, his face heating with embarrassment and incomprehension. "Owun, don't kneel to me. Never again. I mean it."

"But, you worked a miracle, my lord! You're a saint! You're —"

"Stop." Cloud stiffened. How could Owun say something so crazy? Whatever had happened with the cloak — which indeed sounded astonishing — it was impossible that it had anything to do with Cloud. The old man must be the holy one. He was the one wearing it, after all.

"I don't know what you're talking about, but whatever happened, Owun, it was nothing to do with me."

Owun grabbed Cloud's sleeve, trying to pull him in the direction of Paris. "The man told me where to find you. You need to come with me. We need to hurry!"

Cloud resisted, his confusion growing. "Why? Why do you want me to come with you?"

"Tarquin's dying."

Cloud jolted at the unexpected words. But his shock was nothing compared to the thunderbolt that Owun's next sentence sent through him.

"And you need to heal him!"

Chapter Thirty

Cloud couldn't believe this was happening, couldn't believe he was back in Paris. Owun had practically dragged him the whole way. Above all, Cloud couldn't believe the incredible thing his friend was expecting him to do. He wasn't a doctor. He had no power to cure anyone of anything. This was insane. His mind reeled in a swirl of confusion.

As they rounded the corner of the street, they all but collided with a crowd of excited people in front of the nearest house.

"I brought him!" Owun called to the throng, a note of pride in his voice. "Prince Cloud is here!"

Cloud cringed. He was about to shush Owun, to rebuke him for calling him that, but it was too late. Dozens of heads turned. Then, to Cloud's horror, a cheer went up.

"The prince! The holy prince is here!" someone yelled.

"He's going to work a miracle!" another cried.

"Let him through! Move aside!" Excited shouts volleyed through the crowd. People parted left and right, opening a path to the door.

Cloud had a strange compulsion to flee. He didn't want the praise and recognition that belonged to his former life. And as far as him working miracles, well, that was so ridiculous as to be laughable.

Yet Tarquin was dying and might have mere hours to live. Cloud had never felt affection for the man who'd blabbed his whereabouts to anyone who'd listen — and who, once upon a time, had sent him into a spin of jealousy over Genofeva — but the least Cloud could do was pray at the dying man's bedside. Christian charity demanded as much. Besides, Owun had already lugged him all this way to Paris, so he might as well go inside the house.

He glanced at Owun. "Why are all these people here? Are they his friends?"

"No. Most don't know him. But everyone heard about your glowing cloak and knew I was bringing you."

Mortified, Cloud's face heated. If this crowd had gathered to see a miracle, they were going to be disappointed. He was about to object, but never got a chance, because at that moment a blur in a brown dress and flying pigtails barreled out the door and flung herself at his feet.

"My lord prince, you came! Oh thank God, you came!" Genofeva's voice cracked. She looked up at him, her face damp, her anxious eyes imploring. "*Please* do something! Tarq's going to die!"

That's when Cloud noticed her bump. His mind groped for comprehension. Genofeva was pregnant! But, but . . . *How could this be? Who —?*

The realization came in a heartbeat. And even though Cloud had given his life to God, and would want it no other way, something deep inside him gave a tiny lurch of pain.

"Please cure him. Our baby needs him to live."

Cloud knew there was nothing he could do to save her husband, but seeing her sorrow was unbearable.

"Bring me to him," he said gently. "All I can do is pray."

* * * * *

"Tarq, can you hear me? Everything will be alright now. Prince Cloud is here. He's going to heal you."

Cloud had the sensation of moving in a dream. A bad dream. Not only was everyone expecting him to do the impossible, but his emotions jumbled together and tangled his insides in knots. Feelings about Genofeva which he thought he'd overcome years ago attacked with vengeance out of nowhere. The crowd of curious gawkers didn't help. Bodies pressed into the small room, sucking the air out. Between that and the rancid odor of sickness, Cloud felt lightheaded. All he wanted was to escape.

Jesus, he silently pleaded, *help me through this.*

As soon as the prayer shot from his heart, instant peace settled over him. A sensation of God's love pounded through his chest. Christ was close. Invisible, yes, but so very close that Cloud felt like he could reach out and touch Him.

Cloud forced himself to focus on the bed, forbidding himself to look at Genofeva. She belonged to Tarquin. And Cloud belonged to God. Tarquin lay unconscious. His skin had a bluish tinge and sweat drenched him. If not for the occasional rising and falling of his chest, Cloud would believe death had already claimed him. Owun was right; nothing but a miracle could possibly save his life now.

A woman said, "He's been like this for over a week. The doctors say it's hopeless."

Cloud glanced at the woman. In a peasant's dress and middle-aged, she had an arm around Genofeva's shoulders. A man stood behind them, lines of worry creasing his brow. But both looked at Cloud in the same awestruck way. These must be Genofeva's and Owun's parents, the ones who'd seen the stupendous heavenly light from his cloak last night. They mistakenly believed it had something to do with Cloud.

Cloud drew a breath. "Well," he said, "let's pray. God is almighty. He can do anything." He lowered himself to his knees beside the bed and took Tarquin's limp hand. Thumping and bumping filled the room for a moment as the throng of onlookers dropped to their knees as well.

Cloud prayed with all his might. "Dear God in Heaven, Genofeva needs a father for their baby. Please, I beg Thee through the merits and power of Thy Son Jesus Christ, to restore Thy servant Tarquin to full health, if it's Thy loving will."

The limp hand he held grew warm. Life and strength suddenly seemed to pulse through Tarquin. He sputtered a few breaths, then sat upright in bed. A collective gasp shuddered through the room. A few people leapt from their knees and stepped back. Fear and wonder tangibly charged the air.

Tarquin looked around, blinking and dazed. As everyone watched, his complexion returned to a normal color. He stared at Cloud for a second, confused, then took in the crowd gathered around his bed. He frowned. "Wha —? What happened? Why are all these people in my —" He must have suddenly recognized Cloud, because he stopped mid-sentence and demanded, *"You? What are you doing in my house?"*

Without warning, Genofeva shot across the room and crashed into Cloud. The next second he was suffocated in a sweet-scented hug. A rush of longing memories — ones he didn't want — flowed over him. "You healed him! Thank you, oh thank you! Our baby will have –"

He frantically ripped himself away, his heart beating fast. Innocent and impulsive though her hug may be, he found it strange that it was to him, and not her husband, that Genofeva had flown. More than ever now he wanted to flee, to escape this crowded room, to run to the church and adore God in silence for this miracle.

But it was impossible to leave. Suddenly everyone was reaching for him, trying to touch him. Several people fell on their knees at his feet. The place erupted into cacophony.

"A miracle!"

"He worked a miracle!"

"We have a saint in our midst!"

"Quickly, go tell everyone! Hurry!"

"Hurry!"

Everyone was babbling at once.

"Please pray for —"

"My son is sick. Come with me please and —"

"My neighbor broke his arm. Will you —"

"Please, my grandmother —"

Hands were grabbing him, tugging him in every direction.

"Someone bring the bishop! He needs to know!"

The door banged open then shut as a couple boys raced from the room. Cloud could hear their shouts outside. "Prince Cloud of Orleans! He's come back! He's working miracles!"

Someone snatched his habit and Cloud felt a tug, then heard a rip. Part of the material had been snipped off. Immediately other people clutched at his clothes, grappling for pieces as if they were relics.

"Stop!" Cloud begged. He raised his arms, fending them off, trying to back away. "It wasn't me! I did nothing! It was the power of Our Lord Jesus Christ!"

As he fought off the onslaught, he became aware of noises outside. The clomping of many horses. Shouted commands. A commotion of some sort was developing outside Tarquin's house.

The door crashed open with a bang and one of the boys, whom Cloud had seen run out a few moments ago, breathlessly barged back inside. His frantic words silenced the room with the speed of a deadly arrow.

But his words did more than that. They made Cloud's blood run cold.

For the boy was yelling, "King Childebert is here! And he's right outside!"

Chapter Thirty-One

Everyone froze. Cloud could only guess how frightened the people were of Uncle Childebert. His cruelty was known far and wide. Cloud knew it first-hand. He suspected others in this room had experienced it too. If Cloud hadn't already been the center of unwanted attention, he would have become so now. In the fearful silence that fell, all eyes turned to him. Obviously long hair and clothes embroidered with gold weren't needed for these people to expect him to resume his royal role. But if they thought he could protect them from the king, they were out of luck.

Yet Cloud doubted that Uncle Childebert's business was with any of these peasants. Owun had told him this morning that news of his cloak had spread through Paris. It wasn't unreasonable that word had reached the castle. Uncle Childebert would know Cloud was nearby and be looking for him. And the shouting boys in the street just now had blasted his whereabouts to anyone within range.

The boy who'd run back inside confirmed it. "The king demands to see you, my lord."

Owun and Genofeva shot him looks of alarm. Dread wedged beneath Cloud's rib cage like a heavy stone. But his first priority was to keep these people safe, and if he didn't obey the king and go outside, the soldiers might barge in. Innocent bystanders could get hurt.

Reminding himself that God was in control no matter what happened, Cloud breathed a prayer for courage and made his way across the room. This time the people let him go. No more grabbing hands, no more jostling to rip off snippets of his habit, no more requests to cure a loved one. Just tense, cowering silence. The boy in the doorway moved aside so that Cloud could step through.

Footfalls bounded across the floor and someone caught his sleeve from behind. "No, my lord prince! Don't! He'll kill you! Please don't go outside!"

Cloud looked over his shoulder. Genofeva clutched his habit in a death grip.

"If we hurry, Tarq can hide you in our —"

"No." Cloud turned to face her and gently pried her fingers loose. "I'm finished with hiding, Genofeva."

Tears pooled in her impossibly lovely eyes. "I don't want you to die!"

Poor Genofeva. She had such a tender heart.

"It's alright, Genofeva. Don't be sad for me." Cloud forced a smile, then indicated her unborn child. "God has blessed you with so much to look forward to. You have your husband back now, and soon a beautiful baby to take care of. Please don't let anything to do with me mar your happiness."

"But they don't know for sure yet that you're in here. There's still time to —"

"I said *no*, Genofeva."

The firmness in his voice made her flinch, as if he'd slapped her. Cloud instantly felt bad. On impulse, he took her hands in his. "You've been a true friend, Genofeva. The truest kind of friend anyone could have." Across the room, Owun stood protectively in front of his parents. Cloud added, "Both you and your brother. I'm indebted to you forever for what you did all those years ago. Thank you."

Before Genofeva could say anything, Tarquin stormed over and pulled her away. He'd definitely had his full strength restored. He glared at Cloud with obvious jealousy. But there was no reason for Tarquin to worry. Cloud was only too relieved to release Genofeva to a man who could take care of her. Cloud might not have liked Tarquin all those years ago, but he knew that the proud Roman would protect his wife and baby. Not just today, but always. That's all that mattered to Cloud.

Drawing strength from God within him, he turned from the room of quailing onlookers and stepped out the door. No one dared follow.

Dozens of soldiers, mounted and armed, had squeezed into the narrow street, surrounding Tarquin's house. Their horses stamped and snorted. Cloud's muscles tightened. *Why so many men?* Surely Uncle Childebert didn't think he would try to fight? He'd already renounced Orleans; there was no reason for his uncle to bring a small army.

Then again, Uncle Childebert had always thrived on power and attention. Cloud remembered that from his childhood. The more impressive Uncle Childebert could appear, the more fear he pounded into the hearts of his subjects. What better way to intimidate his hated nephew than to show up as if prepared for battle?

Cloud didn't have to scan the warriors to find the king. He spotted him immediately, dressed in royal regalia and mounted on an enormous warhorse in the middle of his men. A safe position. A coward's place.

The second the uncharitable judgment entered Cloud's mind, he was ashamed of himself. It wasn't right to call anyone names, even if it seemed they deserved it. He put his unkind thoughts into Christ's Heart, asking for forgiveness. As in the room a few minutes ago, he felt a burst of peace and knew Jesus was not only near, but *inside him*, watching everything unfold. Whatever the next moments held were in His capable hands. Cloud was perfectly safe.

Although his heart raced, he forced himself to walk calmly towards his uncle. Like the peasants had done earlier, the soldiers reined aside to cut him a path. They could see he was unarmed. He was no threat to their king.

Cloud stopped before the magnificently decked horse, dropped to one knee, and bowed his head. "My lord king. You summoned me."

It wasn't merely in obeisance that he kept his head bowed; it was mostly because he was loath to look at the man who'd helped slay his brothers. True, Uncle Clothaire had been the one who murdered them, not Uncle Childebert. And after Theodoald's death, he *had* argued in favor of Gunther's and Cloud's lives, preferring to toss them in the dungeon rather than kill them. But the part he'd played, luring the boys to his castle knowing they'd be killed, and refusing to save Gunther when it came to the test, was monstrous enough.

Cloud heard the groan of leather as his uncle shifted in the saddle, then there was a swish of heavy material and a thud of boots hitting the ground. Uncle Childebert's legs appeared before him. The same legs that Gunther had been clinging to for dear life when Uncle Clothaire's dagger slammed into his throat. For a horrible moment, raw hatred swelled through Cloud, threatening to overwhelm him. He fought the temptation the only way he knew: head on. Before Satan could overcome him, Cloud looked up, locked eyes with his uncle, and said, "I forgive you. May our infinitely merciful God do the same."

His uncle's eyebrows shot up, the words of forgiveness catching him by surprise. For an awkward moment he glanced around at his troops, his Adam's apple bobbing, as if he suddenly didn't know how to control the situation. Finally he frowned, then said to Cloud, without meeting his gaze, "Get up."

Cloud rose. Unlike when he was nine years old and helpless, he now matched Uncle Childebert in height. In strength, he doubtless surpassed the older man by far. But the king was the one with the sword and the army. Not that it mattered. Cloud had no intention of fighting, even if it had been just the two of them.

Uncle Childebert refused to look Cloud in the eye. Maybe shame prevented him. He cleared his throat and said, "I . . . I came to find you because . . ." He hesitated, as if he had to force his next words. "I wish to grant you land. And funds."

It was Cloud's turn to be speechless. Stunned, he searched the king's face. Was Uncle Childebert repentant? Was this his way of making up for the devastation he'd brought upon Cloud?

Uncle Childebert added in a mumble, "No one of such high birth need beg nor wear rags."

Cloud glanced down at his white habit. It suited him fine. He had no desire to trade it for the clothes of a king. And he wasn't a beggar. He grew his own food and had everything he needed. But he sensed that his uncle was trying to apologize. Maybe a ray of grace had touched his heart and he was sorry for his crimes. After all, he had a saint for a mother, praying for him.

Cloud dipped his head in a bow. "Thank you, my lord. That is most gracious of you."

Land and money. Cloud wanted neither. But the Church was constantly in need of both. And there were always the poor. He would not refuse his uncle's gift.

He raised his head and ventured to ask, "How is Grandmere? Is she well?" Cloud had not seen her since the day they had parted in the woods. So many times he'd thought of going to Lutece to visit her. But he didn't dare, fearful that his presence at her castle might endanger her.

Uncle Childebert's lips closed in a tight line and, again, he looked away. Crimson crept up his neck. "I assume she is fine. I have not seen her in . . ." — he shrugged — "some time." His voice was gruff, ashamed. Cloud felt a pang of sadness for Grandmere. Her own son, and he didn't even care. Was Uncle Clothaire any better? Unlikely.

As for himself, Cloud had never told Grandmere where his hermitage was, hoping thereby to keep her safe. But surely after today, the whereabouts of his humble hut would be blared throughout Gaul. Whatever remained of his hidden life was now gone. As dismaying as that realization was, it meant that Grandmere would be able to find him without danger to herself. A spark of hope flicked through him. He would love to see her again, after all these years!

An idea suddenly came. Grandmere had always loved Saint Martin of Tours, the glorious patron of their land. With the money and land from Uncle Childebert, perhaps Cloud could build a church dedicated to the saint. He could do that for Grandmere, yes. Even if he never saw her again, even if she didn't live to see him build anything, a church to Saint Martin would be a beautiful way to honor her. Cloud made a mental note to ask Bishop Eusebius of Paris for permission.

The king cleared his throat and took a step back, reaching for his stirrup. It signaled the end of their meeting. Cloud almost stopped him, wanting to ask about Charibert, but something inside warned that the mention of his cousin might not be welcome. Especially because Cloud knew that Charibert and Chram were warring against their father. How Uncle Childebert fit into their conflict with Uncle Clothaire, Cloud had no idea.

Without another word, the king swung into his saddle and jerked on the reins. Then he and his army clattered down the street, leaving Cloud not only grateful to be alive, but suddenly a very rich man.

Chapter Thirty-Two

True to Severin's prophecy, the trickle of visitors to Cloud's hermitage turned into not just a stream, but a deluge. After the stir created by his glowing cloak and Tarquin's healing, a day hardly passed without a knock on Cloud's door. Peasants and prelates, beggars and noblemen, clergy and cripples, even little children, braved the lonely forest to find Cloud. Everyone asked for his prayers, his advice, his spiritual counsel — and usually a miracle or two for themselves or a loved one. Cloud couldn't comprehend why they came to him. There were hundreds of priests in Gaul, all much holier and better equipped to guide Christ's flock. And as for the cures, which admittedly had started taking place at his hut, all Cloud did was pray for the sufferers in Jesus's name and by His merits. God alone was responsible for whatever miraculous events occurred; they had absolutely nothing to do with Cloud.

Still, the people kept coming.

Even Uncle Clothaire, to Cloud's amazement, had sent an envoy, gifting Cloud with land and gold almost equal to what Uncle Childebert had given him. Evidently Uncle Clothaire refused to be outdone by his brother. Perhaps grace had touched his cold heart too, making him repent of Theodoald's and Gunther's murders.

That wasn't the only surprise Cloud received lately. The past few weeks a fresh request had started pouring in from his visitors. Men wanted to join Cloud in his way of life. Every week at least one new man showed up, pleading with him to move closer to Paris and start a community of hermits. Cloud was reluctant . . . and overwhelmed. As beautiful an undertaking as that would be, it was definitely a task for a priest, not a prince. And although Cloud's burning desire for the priesthood was deepening day by day, God had not shown him that such was his path.

Despite the now-familiar sounds — cracking twigs, rustling leaves, and occasionally a clomping horse — which always alerted Cloud to the arrival of a visitor, today's noises were unusual. Not only did it sound like half a dozen horses approaching, but Cloud heard rumbling wheels as well. A carriage? With a mounted escort?

Baffled, Cloud rose from the wooden kneeler in the corner of his hut and made his way to the door. The second he opened it, his breath caught.

Abandoning all decorum, Cloud took off across the yard towards the approaching carriage. "Grandmere!"

The driver must have seen Cloud at the same time, for the vehicle lurched to a halt. The carriage door flew open, and, without awaiting assistance, Grandmere jumped out with the agility of a much younger woman, swept up her skirts, and ran to meet Cloud. They collided in a hug.

For a long moment, they held each other. A thousand emotions swirled in Cloud's heart. Words were beyond reach.

Grandmere must've felt the same way. When she finally let him go, she seemed to grope for what to say. She gazed at Cloud with wordless love.

"Grandmere, I can't believe you're here."

Tears moistened her eyes and she took both his hands in hers, squeezing hard. Despite her energetic leap from the carriage a moment ago and the strength of her hug, Cloud could see now how frail and old she was. Worry-lines creased her face, her eyes were pools of deep sadness.

"Cloud," she whispered, "my grandson." Her voice cracked with emotion and she clasped him in another embrace. "I am so proud of you, Cloud. So incredibly proud."

* * * * *

With the exception of three soldiers who insisted on remaining outside the hut, Grandmere had given her escort permission to rest, or take a walk through the peaceful forest if they pleased. No danger lurked in these woods; Cloud was sure Grandmere was safe. Her guard seemed happy to give them privacy. While the two of them sat inside, a few soldiers hiked to the nearest church, a mile or so away, where Cloud went for daily Mass. It hardly surprised him that Grandmere's guards were devout. How could anyone be in contact with her, day after day, and not be affected by her holiness? Impossible.

For the first few minutes, they could only look at each other, too full of emotion to speak. Then the floodgates broke and they began to fill each other in on everything that had happened since their last meeting, so many years ago near the ruins of that ancient stairwell. Yet in spite of Grandmere's joy at seeing him, Cloud detected she was holding something back. The worry in her eyes was not there without reason.

Reaching across the table, he took her wooden cup and walked to his crackling fire. Lifting the blackened pot, the only cooking utensil he owned, he refilled Grandmere's vessel with the sweet herbal brew he'd prepared — one he remembered from his childhood that she loved, and the herbs of which he'd thankfully planted. Should he try to draw out the cause of

163

Grandmere's obvious worry?

"How is Charibert?" He set the steaming drink in front of her and found himself holding his breath. Did he really want to know what was happening with his cousin? Charibert had risked his own life to save Cloud's, and because of that, the two shared a bond that could never be severed. Yet the last time Cloud had seen Charibert, things had not gone well. Was Charibert perhaps the reason for Grandmere's unspoken pain?

Grandmere nursed the cup in trembling hands. "Charibert is . . ." An anguished sigh escaped her. She lowered her eyes and stared at the cup, probably to hide her tears. "Charibert has taken after his father. With the women, I mean. He has so many of them, Cloud. I fear greatly for his soul."

Disappointment ripped through Cloud at her words. He knew impurity was rampant, especially among royalty. Why had he imagined Charibert would end up any different? For all his bravery and self-sacrifice of years ago, Charibert had turned out like the rest of them.

Cloud couldn't help but wonder if he himself would have fallen prey to the same vice, had he grown up in the normal way of princes. God had spared him so much. He hadn't realized it as a child, but now he fully understood that the events of his life had been an incredible proof of God's mercy and love. The sins he could have committed had he been a king! Theodoald and Gunther had been spared too. How good God had been to all three of them!

Grandmere said, "I pray for Charibert so hard. Please pray for him too, Cloud, that someday he returns to God."

"Of course, Grandmere. You know I will." The thought of Charibert going to Hell was a dagger in Cloud's heart. He'd always prayed for Charibert, but now would plead with God with all his might for his cousin's soul. "And Chram?" he asked reluctantly. "What happened to his brother Chram?" Dread curled his insides. Chram would be grown up now. If Charibert caused Grandmere so much grief by his wayward living, how much more her other, much more rebellious, grandson?

Grandmere looked up, startled. "You haven't heard?"

"No."

"Chram died." She blinked back tears. "My son Clothaire murdered him."

Chram's very own father.

"He torched the house Chram was staying in. Burned him to death in his sleep, with his young wife and child."

Good God. Cloud was aghast. "Grandmere, I . . . I'm so sorry." Words failed him. He couldn't even imagine the pain Grandmere felt at such horror, especially because it was done by her own son. The same son who had murdered Theodoald and Gunther. That made three of her grandsons, brutally killed by Uncle Clothaire.

Suddenly Grandmere could hold back her sorrow no longer. Tears spilled from her eyes. "And now they're going to war against each other," she choked out. "They're going to kill each other."

Cloud didn't understand. "Who? Who's going to war?"

Grandmere broke down in sobs. Cloud rushed to her side to comfort her.

"Who, Grandmere?"

"My sons." She could barely speak through her tears. "Tomorrow, Cloud. They're riding into battle against each other."

Cloud's heart stopped. Uncle Clothaire and Uncle Childebert were going to war.

Chapter Thirty-Three

Cloud had known, from the minute Grandmere left, that he wouldn't sleep tonight. How could he allow himself rest when Grandmere's heart was being torn apart by her only remaining sons? She'd already lost her other children. Cloud remembered the story of how her firstborn, Ingomer, had died soon after being baptized. Grandpere Clovis, not yet a Christian at the time, had blamed God for their baby's death, which caused Grandmere untold suffering. Years later, Grandmere's only daughter, Aunt Clotilda, died from abuse at the hands of her monstrous Visigoth husband. As if those two deaths weren't bad enough, Grandmere was forced to witness the severed head of her other son, Cloud's own father, being carried through the countryside on a pike. If that wasn't the stuff of nightmares for a mother, Cloud didn't know what was. And now, Uncle Childebert and Uncle Clothaire, the only two she had left, planned to face each other in battle. If either died by the other's sword tomorrow morning, how could Grandmere bear such grief?

Bracing himself for a night of prayer, Cloud lit a torch, tucked his precious book of Scriptures under his arm, and headed to the nearby church to keep vigil before Jesus in the Blessed Sacrament. Wherever Grandmere was tonight, Cloud had no doubt she would spend the night in prayer, begging God for the safety of her sons. Cloud would join his prayers to hers.

Hardly had he set off when he realized that the firelight from his torch was unnecessary. Bright stars blinked in the cloudless night sky, easily lighting his way through the woods. Extinguishing the flame, Cloud stopped to gaze at the beautiful canopy of Heaven above him. He'd never seen such a clear, peaceful night. The magnificent sight of a million stars took his breath away. How, he wondered, could his uncles plot evil on a night that displayed so wondrously the glory and grandeur of their loving God? The kings' cold hearts were a mystery that Cloud could never understand.

After a few peaceful minutes of allowing himself to be entranced by the twinkling stars, Cloud returned his attention to earth. He was eager to reach the church. By the time the stars above were replaced by the gentle sunrise, his uncles' armies would clash in war.

Only a miracle could stop them.

* * * * *

Somewhere, in the first moments of dawn, Cloud saw her.

It happened with no warning.

One second Cloud was fighting off sleep in the church, trying to hold his wandering thoughts in check as he drowsily gazed at the tabernacle. The next second, Grandmere appeared. In a faraway chapel, before a different tabernacle, miles away. But Cloud saw her as clearly as if she knelt just ahead of him. Only inches from the altar, she clung to the very cloths, all but prostrate with grief. Tears streamed down her cheeks. Pleading, begging, imploring God's mercy with an intensity born of sheer desperation.

Cloud's vision suddenly raced to a meadow. Two armies gathered on opposite sides. The morning sun rose higher in the

167

cloudless sky, reflecting off thousands of swords and shields.

His heart beat faster.

Please Lord. Please, for Grandmere's sake . . .

Grandmere at the altar again. Weeping. Bargaining with Heaven.

The meadow. His uncles shouting orders. Soldiers positioning their horses in battle formation.

Grandmere, collapsing to the chapel floor in grief.

Cloud's heart pounded, ready to explode in his chest. *God, please! Hear Grandmere's prayers! Don't let Uncle Clothaire and Uncle Childebert kill each* — A massive flash of light, followed by a deafening clap of thunder, shuddered through the building, stunning Cloud. He jerked upright as a second bolt of lightning lit up the church where he knelt, shaking it to its very foundation.

He saw his uncles and their armies, miles away, jolt in shock. In the blink of an eye, the bright morning sun had vanished, like a candle blown out. Giant black clouds appeared out of nowhere and swept ominously over the battlefield, blown by a gale force wind. The sky rumbled and cracked, both above the church where Cloud knelt and in the meadow of his vision. Lightning hit the ground between the two opposing armies with a terrifying flare.

Horses skittered and bolted in fear. Uncle Childebert was thrown from his saddle. Uncle Clothaire galloped away in panic. The ground trembled all around them with lightning strikes and earsplitting thunder. Cloud saw it all, as clearly as if he stood in the field. Chaos erupted, scattering both armies.

Then the sky opened wide, unleashing torrential rain.

Chapter Thirty-Four

Cloud knew a messenger would come to his hut, eventually, with the news. But he didn't need to hear it from anyone. He'd watched Grandmere Clothilde die, far away, after the failed battle, and he knew she'd offered her life to Jesus in exchange for the lives of her two sons. The miraculous storm that prevented Uncle Clothaire and Uncle Childebert from killing each other was God's answer to her prayers. Grandmere Clothilde had done it. *Saint* Clothilde had done it. How Cloud loved her!

To his surprise, he felt no grief at her passing. He had witnessed her pure soul soar straight to Heaven, where she rested now in God's infinite love. Her heart could never again be pierced by her wicked children. Everything inside Cloud swelled with joy at her happiness.

Besides, Grandmere was near. Of that he was sure. She would cheer him on, now more than ever, to stay part of *The Gang*.

Despite all that, he figured he'd better be at his hermitage when a messenger came. So he'd reluctantly left the presence of the Blessed Sacrament and returned to his hut to await news.

It was evening by the time he heard the clomping of hooves.

He hurried outside to greet the messenger.

Cloud blinked in surprise when he saw the man. It was a priest.

How strange. Why would a priest bring news of Grandmere's death? Cloud had assumed that someone from her castle would come. Had word spread that quickly among the clergy? It had only been a few hours.

He lengthened his stride across the yard towards the horse.

The priest waved in greeting. His smile stretched wide. "Good prince," he called, "I bring you most happy news."

Happy? Well, yes. For Cloud. He'd seen Grandmere fly to Heaven. But normally an announcement of death wasn't considered happy. Yet, oddly, the priest was grinning ear to ear.

Cloud reached him. "I already know."

"You do?" The priest pulled his horse to a halt and frowned, as if confused.

"About my grandmother," Cloud said.

"Your . . . grandmother?"

"Yes."

The man looked so baffled that Cloud added, "Queen Clothilde."

The priest's frown deepened and he scratched his head. "I don't know anything about the queen. I bring a message from Bishop Eusebius."

It was Cloud's turn to be confused. The bishop of Paris had sent him? Really? This wasn't about Grandmere's death?

"The bishop has a message for me?"

"Indeed." The other's smile returned, full force. "He bids you come to Paris immediately, that you may be ordained a priest."

Ordained a priest. Cloud's greatest dream. He was speechless.

Another bidding, so similar in wording, yet a world apart, flashed through his memory.

'They bid thee send the boys immediately, that they may be made kings.'

A senator. Grandmere's autumn garden. A rumbling carriage. A lifetime ago.

And now. All these pain-filled years later, a crown was again held out to Cloud from Paris. A true crown. An everlasting crown. A crown that could never be wrested away, a crown that bloodshed could never steal.

The holy priesthood. Cloud's deepest desire. The highest honor any man could possibly receive from Christ.

Cloud raised his eyes towards Heaven, and could almost swear he saw Grandmere Clothilde wink at him.

Thank you, Grandmere.

A new life, a beautiful life, was about to begin.

Epilogue

Gaul, 561 A.D.

"Grand-mama, are you alright? Why are you crying?"

Startled from her thoughts, Genofeva looked at her three-year-old grandson kneeling beside her. She hadn't realized a teardrop was sliding down her cheek. She swiped it away with the back of her hand and blinked back the rest that threatened to escape. Forcing a smile, she whispered back, "I'm alright, sweetie. I'm just crying because . . ." She tried to think of something that wouldn't upset little Martin. ". . . because this church is so beautiful."

It wasn't a lie. The Church of Saint Martin of Tours was magnificent. Not in a showy way, like perhaps another prince would have built to flaunt his wealth. But in a simple, humble way, perfectly reflecting her lord prince's heart and his burning love for Christ in the Blessed Sacrament. Whenever Genofeva had free time, she plodded the long road to come here to pray. It made her feel so close to God. And, well . . . to *him*.

That wasn't wrong, was it? Cloud was in Heaven, after all. Saints were meant to be loved. Genofeva could admit it, now that she was widowed and wise and brutally honest, that her feelings for Cloud hadn't always been because of his holiness. Before she married Tarq — and even for a long time after, if she were perfectly truthful with herself — she'd been swept off her feet by everything about the handsome young prince. But she'd always known, from their very first meeting in her parents' woodshed, that their worlds could never entwine. Marrying him was nothing but a fantasy of a silly peasant girl. In a funny way it had made things easier when she'd witnessed him renounce his kingdom in order to follow Christ. That's when Genofeva knew without a doubt that Cloud had been claimed by Jesus alone. And who was she to interfere with *that*?

Besides, Tarq had treated her decently. He hadn't proved easy to live with during the eighteen years they'd been together, but he'd given her a safe home, a beautiful daughter, and now the joy of a grandchild. Genofeva couldn't complain.

"Is this the Martin I'm named after?" For the second time, her grandson's voice sliced through her wandering thoughts.

"Yes, sweetie."

"Can we leave now?" He stood up, tugging her sleeve. "I want to see great-uncle Owun."

Genofeva smiled. "Of course." She was anxious to visit her brother too. Hopefully they'd catch him between his many prayers. Martin pulled her to her feet and yanked her towards the door. "But we have to be quiet near his hut, Martin. His brother-hermits might be praying."

"I will, Grand-mama," Martin said in nearly a shout.

Genofeva laughed and let him haul her outside.

The countryside had changed so much from her childhood. Crop-heavy fields replaced what had once been forest. Humble hermitages, built by the countless men whom Cloud had inspired to give their lives to God, clustered around the church. Wayside shrines dotted the meadows. The prince-turned-priest had worked untiringly for God's glory in his nearly forty years upon earth, and everywhere Genofeva looked, he'd left some beautiful mark of his passing. Not even to mention the miracles! Cloud worked miracles galore, both before his death and after. All these stupendous graces were flung across the land because of her wonderful friend, Prince Cloud.

How could Genofeva be sad? Part of her mourned him, yes. All of Gaul had been grieved by his death last year. But Genofeva knew that her gentle lord prince would be waiting for her in Heaven. Not only her. The saint would be waiting for all those who prayed to him, throughout future centuries. The thought was amazing to Genofeva and instantly lifted her heart. She had a powerful and loving intercessor in Heaven. How wonderful was that?

On impulse, she tossed her graying braids over her shoulders, hiked up the hem of her dress, and threw Martin a mischievous grin. "Race you to great-uncle Owun's hermitage!"

Laughing, she took off at a run, her grandson at her heels.

Who knows, she thought as her bare feet flew over the flower-strewn meadow . . . Maybe she would leave the world and become a hermit too.

And why not?

Far stranger things had happened in this blessed land of Gaul.

Prayer to Saint Cloud

O God, Who, by the gift of the priesthood and the splendor of his virtues, didst

glorify Blessed Cloud, humbling himself for Thy sake upon earth, grant us by

his example to minister worthily unto Thee, and by his intercession ever to

advance in merit and grace. Through Christ Our Lord. Amen.

Saint Cloud is also known as Saint Clodoald.

His feast day is September 7.

Saint Clothilde's feast day is June 3.

Did you know that reviews help sell books?

If you have enjoyed this novel, or any of Susan Peek's books, please consider

leaving a brief review on Amazon or Goodreads.

Thank you, and God bless!